Hope Springs™

THE VIRTUE CHRONICLES

THE
SAINTLY
OUTLAW

Hope Springs™

THE VIRTUE CHRONICLES

THE
SAINTLY
OUTLAW

By Paul McCusker

AUGUSTINE INSTITUTE
Greenwood Village, CO

Augustine Institute

6160 S. Syracuse Way, Suite 310

Greenwood Village, CO 80111

Tel: (866) 767-3155

www.augustineinstitute.org

Cover Design: Christina Gray

ISBN 978-1-7338598-7-5
Library of Congress Control Number 2019941585

Printed in Canada

Adapted with gratitude from the works of Henry Gilbert and through the generosity of the Palmer Family.

THE
SAINTLY
OUTLAW

PROLOGUE

It all started just before Christmas when Andrew Perry's family went Christmas shopping in downtown Hope Springs. They weren't there as part of the crowds of tourists who came from Denver and the other bigger towns to find some bargains or reasonably priced antiques. The Perrys lived in Hope Springs.

Andrew had gone off on his own to look for presents. His first priority was to go to the Pen & Paint Art Store to find some pens, pencils, and art supplies for his sister Lizzy.

He was walking along, looking in the shop windows, when he passed the Old Bank Building. That's what all the locals called it: "The Old Bank Building," even though it had stopped being a bank building sometime back in the 1970s when the state and national banks opened branches in other parts of town. The bank—the Hope Springs Bank & Trust—closed down and the building was abandoned. Small businesses used it from time to time, and even the City Hall was housed there when work

1

was being done on the real City Hall. After a while, a family with a personal interest in the place bought the whole building and restored it as a giant antique shop.

Andrew had been past the Old Bank Building a lot of times, but he'd hardly paid attention to it. But this time something caught his eye and he stopped.

He realized the front of the building was the exact same image that had been painted on the front of his family's Advent calendar.

The Perry family's Advent calendar had been in the family for almost a hundred years. It was made of wood and stood about three feet tall and was half-a-foot thick. The front was painted to look like a red brick building and had large windows on the bottom and a big door and smaller windows going up for three stories. The windows were made with little hinges that opened up to small compartments to reveal the Advent surprises.

Theodore Perry, Andrew's grandfather (well, he had a couple of "greats" in front of "grandfather," but Andrew could never remember how many) had built the Advent calendar for his kids back in the 1920s. It was handed down from generation to generation and wound up with Andrew's dad.

Andrew always felt a small surge of pride when his family set up the Advent calendar for the season. People who visited often commented on how amazing it was. It was unique.

But Andrew now saw that it wasn't unique at all. There, right in front of him, was the real thing: the Old Bank

Building was the model for the Perry Advent Calendar. And there, in the picture window of the Old Bank Building, was an Advent calendar just like the one Andrew had at home.

Andrew couldn't believe it. There it was, on display standing on fake snow, dwarfed by a huge Christmas tree made of silver pine needles, with a multicolored spinning wheel that slowly turned in front of a bright bulb to change the color of the tree. The entire spectacle was lined with old-fashioned Christmas garlands and lights with gigantic bulbs.

What is this place doing with our Advent calendar? he wondered.

He stepped back and looked up at the sign above the door. Bold black cursive letters announced: *The Virtue Curiosity Shoppe*. (The word "shop" really had an extra "p" and "e" at the end. Andrew assumed that whoever did the sign took the spelling from a Charles Dickens story.)

Andrew thought, *It's a curiosity shop and now I'm curious*, so he went through the double doors.

"Sensory overload" was the phrase that came to his mind as he entered. The vast room that greeted him must have been the lobby to the old bank, but now the entire area looked like a department store for antiques. Racks and stands held old-fashioned dresses, suits, and all kinds of hats: hats with feathers, stove-pipe hats, and hats shaped like plates. Old furniture had been arranged as dining rooms, kitchens, bedrooms, and living rooms. There were glass cabinets and lamps and vases and old dial telephones and wooden toys. Dark wooden cases were gathered in clusters, their shelves cluttered with leather books and knickknacks and lots of things Andrew didn't recognize. He heard a tinkling sound and looked up. A giant chandelier hung from the ceiling, reaching down at least two stories with a gold chain.

Closed doors lined some of the other walls. Open doors led to more rooms with smaller displays of antiques. One was filled with Christmas decorations. He noticed a long counter in the back that sat on marble pedestals and had small iron windows. He was pretty sure the bank tellers had worked there.

Andrew hadn't moved from the front door. He'd been standing there, his mouth hanging open, slowly taking in all he could see. Suddenly, something clicked next to him. He turned to see an upright piano. "Silent Night" started to play all by itself. The keys moved without fingers touching them.

"That's our player piano," a woman's voice said.

Andrew spun around to see a woman standing behind a broad counter to the side of the front door. It was the kind of counter he'd seen in a fancy old western hotel, with panels of gold and red velvet on the front and a polished wood top. There was even a large silver bell on the counter to summon a clerk.

"Have you ever seen one?" The woman had a friendly smile and round silver glasses framing her big brown eyes. Her brown hair was piled in a loose bun on top of her head. She came around the counter to the piano and pointed to two panels on the front above the keyboard.

She slid them aside to reveal a wide scroll that was rolling down. The scroll had holes all over it. She explained, "There is a mechanism inside that moves the scroll. The holes in the scroll trigger the levers inside that move the keys and play the music."

"Like an old computer," Andrew said, looking closer at the scroll.

The woman pulled her glasses down the bridge of her nose and looked at Andrew. "You are one of the Perry kids," she said.

Andrew nodded.

She smiled and said, "I knew it!" She put out her hand for Andrew to shake. "I'm sure you don't remember me. I'm Catherine Drake. I went to school with your father. You were a lot younger the last time you came into my store. I saw you from time to time when your family came for summer visits."

Andrew could never forget his summer visits to Hope Springs. His father had grown up in the town but went off to college in Denver and later founded a successful computer programming business. The family had lived in Denver until the previous summer, when Andrew's parents decided it was time to move to Hope Springs for good.

Mrs. Drake put a finger to her chin and tapped lightly. "It's you and your younger sister and ... the twins," she said.

"Yes, ma'am," Andrew said. "Lizzy, Nick, and Sam."

She looked at Andrew's face and slowly shook her head. "You look just like him, you know."

"Like who?" Andrew asked, thinking she was likely talking about his dad.

She turned and pointed. Dominating a section of a far wall was a massive painting in a gold frame. In the painting stood two men dressed in old-fashioned suits, the kind with long jackets and big collars and vests and ties. Both men had their hands on an oversized globe of the world.

"Take a closer look," Mrs. Drake said and gestured for Andrew to walk over. "The man with the moustache and gold wire-framed glasses there on the left is Alfred Virtue. He founded the bank."

Andrew had heard of the man, maybe in school. Or maybe his parents had mentioned him. His eyes went to the man on the right.

"That's Theodore Perry," she said.

Andrew let out a small gasp. Theodore Perry looked like an older version of Andrew. Or maybe Andrew looked like a younger version of Theodore Perry. He wasn't sure which way to think about it.

"Alfred Virtue was my great-great-grandfather. I always get confused about how many 'greats' he was," Mrs. Drake said.

"Me too," Andrew said.

"Alfred Virtue and Theodore Perry were best friends and business partners."

Andrew gazed at the painting and suddenly felt as if all the antiques and clothes and displays had been cleared away and there was Theodore Perry, live and in-person, standing in the bank with customers, all dressed in clothes of that time. The bank tellers stood in their stations behind the iron grates on the long counter, with customers passing slips of paper or receiving money. Their voices echoed inside, and from outside came the sounds of horses clip-clopping along the street. Through the big front window, Andrew saw the carriages and wagons and even a black Model T car, whose driver was scowling as he tried to navigate around the slow traffic. A police officer in a blue uniform, twirling a big nightstick, walked toward him.

It was so vivid that Andrew had to blink a few times to check himself. Then, in an instant, the scene was gone and he was standing back in the Curiosity Shoppe with "Silent Night" playing from the piano and the normal traffic moving outside.

"Are you all right?" Mrs. Drake asked, looking at him with a puzzled expression.

Andrew would later try to think about how that moment triggered something inside of him. He had a powerful desire to go *into* that painting, into the moment when the two men posed for the painter. He wanted to stand in that room as it once was. He wanted to pick up the antiques all around the room, not just to hold them, but to experience them as they were when they weren't considered antiques. He wanted to feel what it was like to live in the past.

"I could stay here all day," Andrew heard himself say to her.

She smiled at him and said, "I know what you mean."

Just then, other customers came in. Mrs. Drake said, "Excuse me," and went off to talk to them.

Andrew wasn't sure where to begin with such a huge shop. He slowly turned in a circle to take it all in. That's when he saw something move behind the old bank counter. A girl appeared in one of the teller's slots. She had a round face and round glasses and short dark hair. He figured she was his age.

She saw him looking back at her and ducked down.

Weird, he thought. He wondered if she was related to Mrs. Drake. Or maybe she worked there. Or, worse, she might be sneaking around. *Should I say something to Mrs. Drake, just in case?* he thought.

Just then Andrew's little sister Sam was at his side. "Hi, Andrew!" she called out.

The rest of his family had come in when Andrew wasn't paying attention.

"Hi," he said to her and followed her back to the front door. Andrew's dad and Mrs. Drake talked like old friends and even discussed the painting and how much Andrew looked like Theodore Perry. The burst of chat and interest in the shop took Andrew away, though he kept seeing the mystery girl out of the corner of his eye. She kept peering from behind the clothes racks and bookcases. He wondered why she was watching them. Then he realized that she was watching *him*.

His dad said it was time to go and everyone was walking out when Mrs. Drake leaned down and said to Andrew quietly, "Come back any time you want."

He nodded.

She added in a whisper, "Alfred and Ted were up to some really interesting things. You should see what's in the basement some time."

Andrew would think much later, *That was the start of the adventure.*

It was April in Hope Springs, which didn't mean it was springtime yet, since the Rocky Mountains were known for quick changes in the weather. One day it might be 60 degrees with buds appearing on the trees, the next day it could be 34 degrees with a foot of snow on the ground. On this particular day, Andrew was wearing a heavier coat because, though the sun was bright, there was an arctic wind blowing through the town.

Andrew didn't mind. He enjoyed the unpredictability of the weather.

He opened the door to the Virtue Curiosity Shoppe and stepped in. The Christmas displays in the window were of course gone. Catherine Drake had replaced them with antique shelves lined with first editions of classic works of literature, all in leather bindings and a few opened up to show off the colorful artwork inside.

Andrew had been to the shop a few times since Christmas. He liked to look around at all the antiques and wander through the rooms. He was especially interested in the collection of local history books, many that told stories of the town's legends. His ancestors were mentioned a few times.

The girl he'd seen at Christmas was sometimes there. But she did what she'd done before: watch him from behind the displays and the furniture in a game of hide-and-seek.

Finally, he had asked Catherine Drake who the girl was.

She gave him a knowing smile. "That's my niece," she had said. "Evangeline, but we call her Eve." She cupped her hands around her mouth and called out, "*Eeeee-v.*"

Eve didn't answer. A door slammed somewhere in the back of the shop.

"*Eve Virtue!*" Catherine Drake had called out again. She gave Andrew an apologetic look. "I don't know why she's being so shy."

On this particular Saturday morning, Catherine Drake said hello as Andrew walked in and she directed him to a section in the far-right corner with some new history books she'd recently picked up from a family estate. "It's near the old teller counter," she said.

Andrew made his way past the tables and displays and found the collection of books. He had just picked up one about Native American tribes in the area when he saw a face looking at him through the bars of one of the teller stations.

He sighed. It was Eve Virtue playing her game again.

He looked directly at her, but she didn't hide this time. She held steady and gazed at him.

Her face wasn't as round as he remembered, and she wasn't wearing the round glasses, but her hair was still short in a pixie style and he now realized it was almost jet-black. But it was her eyes that caught his attention. They were like a color he had never seen: pale blue and green, maybe, but not exactly. They shone bright, even though the corner was in a shadow.

"Aren't we a little too old for hide-and-seek?" he said to her.

Eve smiled and dropped down behind the counter. Andrew put down the book and took a few steps to see where she'd gone. He saw her crouched down, moving along the back wall like a cat past the doors to the different rooms. Then she ducked inside one, leaving the door open.

Andrew slowly followed her, not sure if he was supposed to or even if he wanted to. Then he heard a clock chime from inside the room. Then another. And another.

He peeked around the door. The girl was standing in the middle of the room. He saw only now that she wore a dark blue sweater, light-colored blue jeans, and gray sneakers. She was waiting for him, that smile still in place. She lifted her right hand to the base of her neck. She clasped something in her fist that was attached to a thin silver chain.

The chimes increased, singing in high and low notes, and Andrew realized the room was filled with clocks. All kinds of clocks: large and small, of different shapes and colors, sitting on tables and shelves and hanging on the walls without any clear order. Grandfather clocks stood proudly like soldiers along one wall. The biggest of them was in the far corner, as tall as the ceiling. It had a giant face that glowed yellow and a door as big as one you'd find on a closet.

The clocks were chiming eleven o'clock. But Andrew noticed the giant clock was showing one o'clock. He waited for the chimes to stop, then asked the girl, "Why do you keep playing hide-and-seek?"

"I had to be sure," she said. "I wanted to know if you are serious."

"Serious about what?"

"The past."

"What past?"

"The past."

"What are you talking about?"

"Are you serious, Andrew Perry?" It was the first time she'd said his name.

"Serious about *what*, Eve Virtue?" he mimicked her.

"An amazing mystery."

"I like mysteries," he said, thinking about stolen money and murders and weird creatures from outer space.

She said, "Decide now."

"Decide *what?*"

"If you're coming or not," she said. She turned and went to the giant clock with the huge door. The door had a key in the lock. She pulled it out and held it up for him to see. It was an old-fashioned skeleton key. "It took me a long time to figure out what this key went to," she said. "Alfred Virtue has a lot of keys hidden around."

She put the key into the lock again and gave it a hard turn. The latch clicked loudly. She pulled the door open.

Andrew stepped forward to get a better view. He saw the pendulum inside swinging back and forth in slow, wide movements. Behind the pendulum was dark space. He squinted but couldn't see the back of the clock.

"Coming?" she asked.

The pendulum swung far to the right. To Andrew's surprise, Eve jumped past it and into the darkness.

It can't be that big, he thought. He peered into the clock cabinet. A black nothing peered back at him. *Is there an opening in the back of the clock to a secret room or a tunnel?*

Eve laughed from somewhere inside.

"Don't be afraid," she said. Her voice echoed like she was in a big room.

"I'm *not*," he called back to her, annoyed at the suggestion.

She said impatiently, "Then *let's go!*"

Andrew waited until the pendulum swung past and jumped through.

He took a few steps and then stopped. Pitch-black. He looked back and could see the swinging pendulum and the light from the room of clocks. But he couldn't see anything ahead of or around him.

"Hello?" he called out. His voice echoed, as if he stood in a vast space. "If you jump out to scare me, I'm leaving," he said.

"Come on," she said. Her voice was somewhere ahead—*far* ahead.

"This is creepy," he said to the vast darkness. "How big is this place?"

He imagined he was in a big warehouse, maybe a stock room where Catherine Drake stored a lot of the antiques.

"Walk straight," Eve called out. She sounded even farther away.

He held his hands in front of him and began to walk slowly. He feared bumping into something hard. "Where's the light?" he asked, but she didn't answer. The room went on and on. He turned to look behind him again. The pendulum and light from the room were like a distant window.

He hadn't taken *that* many steps.

"Come on," Eve said, startling him. She sounded like she was only a foot away, though he still couldn't see her. She took hold of his hand.

Suddenly, bright colored lights shot past them to the left and right, over their heads and below their feet, like they were surging forward—except they were not moving. The *lights* were. He saw Eve in silhouette against the speeding lights. She was looking ahead. Then she let go of his hand and the lights went out.

It was dark again. *But not the same kind of dark*, Andrew thought. *More like a gray.*

He was aware of the sound of birds. He also felt as if the air had become heavy, like it did on really humid days. And there was a smell that reminded him of grass after it had been cut. *It smells green*, he thought.

He saw a vertical line of light flickering just ahead. It reminded him of the sun shining through the middle of closed curtains.

Was it a stage curtain? he wondered. *Did Catherine Drake set up some kind of historical presentation? Am I about to walk into a show?*

He shoved his hands into the vertical line of light and pushed the curtains aside. Only, they weren't cloth curtains. They were wooden and bristly, scratching the backs of his hands and rustling with the sounds of leaves and branches.

He emerged into a new light and had to blink a few times to adjust his eyes.

He froze where he was. He couldn't believe what he was seeing.

Spread out in front of Andrew was a forest, a *large* forest with countless trees and a golden haze of sunlight mixing with the greens and browns.

He thought hard and couldn't connect what he was seeing with what he knew to be reality. There was a parking lot behind Virtue's Curiosity Shoppe, not a forest. And, as he looked, it occurred to him that this wasn't the kind of forest he knew in Colorado, with slender pine trees and stick-like branches and needles on the ground and the kind of crisp air that came with being high above sea level. These trees were fat and had knotholes and branches reaching out like muscular arms. The air was thick with the smell of damp leaves and moss.

He thought hard about it some more. *It's a virtual display*, he decided, *like they have in museums and amusement parks. I'm looking at a 3-D screen in front of me and they have machines doing tricks with the light and making the air feel like it does.*

To prove he was right, he took a few steps forward. He came to a tree and touched the bark. It was rough. An ant marched near his finger.

He looked up. The tree reached high. Through the branches he could see blue sky and white clouds. A bird darted past.

Turning around, he looked at the curtain he'd passed through. It was actually heavy vines covering the mouth of a cave.

He thought, *This is amazing technology!*

He considered going back, just to see if the cave was a warehouse, but the shout of a man stopped him. He turned to look. Off to the right, someone or something was racing through the trees. Whatever it was ran in his direction.

He heard shouts and then dogs barking and, coming closer, the sound of a low snarling and snorting, like a really angry pig.

Then he saw it. A big black hairy beast with a long face and tusks on each side of its snout. And it was running straight for him.

He didn't know what to do. If it was a virtual machine, the beast would run through him. But his instincts said to get out of the way—*and fast.*

Andrew staggered backward a few steps, looking around. He half-ran several more steps.

"Up here."

He stopped and looked up. Eve was stretched out on a thick tree branch.

"You better hurry," she said. "That boar will trample you."

He ran over to the tree and jumped for the lowest branch. Catching hold, he pulled himself up and scrambled higher until he was on a branch near her.

"They'll be chasing it," she said. "Keep quiet. We mustn't let them know we're here."

"*Who?*" Andrew asked.

She put a finger to her lips and pointed down.

The boar was underneath them now, moving in a small circle, unsure of where to run. Dogs came from different directions and quickly had it surrounded. They snarled and barked at the beast, their hair high on their backs. The boar squealed and snorted, darting back and forth between the dogs. It charged at one with its tusks. With a yelp, the dog stumbled back, then fell to its side, whining as blood poured out of a gash.

Andrew heard a sharp buzzing sound. The boar shrieked as an arrow hit it in the neck. It shrieked furiously and circled in a frenzy. A spear struck its right side. Then another arrow flew from yet another direction, joining the spear. Then a spear caught the left side of its body. The boar dropped, its legs kicking. It made a loud and horrible noise as it lay dying.

None of this makes sense, Andrew thought. *It can't be virtual reality.*

Four men appeared below and kicked at the dogs to move them aside, then stepped up to the squirming animal.

Though they were below him, Andrew was at enough of an angle to make out their features. One man was older, with silver hair and a matching beard. He wore a dark blue robe with gold trim laced with patterns Andrew couldn't see very well. A gold belt of chains hung loose around his waist. Black shoes peeked out from under his robe.

Two of the other men were younger, each with dark curly hair. One had a short beard and the other was clean-shaven. They wore tunics, one red and the other purple, that also had gold trim with the same kinds of patterns that the older man wore. Their legs were covered with dark leggings, though one wore brown leather boots that folded down at the top. The other wore dark shoes that looked like slippers.

There was a fourth man in a plain brown tunic that went down to his knees. A belt that looked like a rope was tied in the middle of his waist. He wore leggings like the other men, though his were dirty and torn. His brown shoes had leather straps that held them together.

The whole scene reminded Andrew of a medieval fair his parents had taken him to one summer.

The squirming boar made another terrible squeal.

Animatronics, Andrew hoped. *Some kind of robot.* But the blood looked very real.

He glanced at Eve. She was still watching the men.

The silver-haired man came nearest to the boar. He raised a sword high and brought it point-down into the chest of the beast. The boar stopped squirming.

The two young men laughed as the older man handed his sword to the fourth man, clearly a servant. "Clean that," he said. He gestured to the dead boar. "Get this back to the house. Put it on the spit for dinner."

"Yes, my lord," the fourth man said.

The whining dog caught the older man's attention. "Stop that," he said.

The clean-shaven, curly-haired man drew a knife from his belt and, with one swift stroke, silenced the dog.

The servant put his fingers to his mouth and let off a loud shrill whistle. Andrew heard voices and footfalls crashing through the forest. Through the branches of his hiding place, he saw a dozen men, dressed like the servant, rushing toward them.

The three men walked away, but the dogs moved in to smell the dead boar. The older man gave a shout and the dogs broke away to follow. Soon, the servants arrived with a carrier made of wooden slats. With grunts and gasps, they began the work of loading the boar and carting it away.

The forest fell into a peaceful silence. Eve beckoned Andrew to follow her. She scampered like a squirrel along the branch, then up to another that stretched across to an adjacent tree. She paused there and waved for him to hurry.

Carefully, he did what she had done. The branches were thick enough not to shake very much. He gained his footing and grew more confident as he went.

Eve led the way, crawling from one branch to another, finding ones that bridged to another tree and then another.

Andrew struggled to keep up. *Now I feel like I'm in a Tarzan movie*, he thought.

Everything his senses experienced—the humid air, the rough bark of the trees, the effort to keep balanced—told him that it was all real, but his brain couldn't make sense of it. How could a 3-D image or virtual reality program or a stage show be this *real*?

"This way," Eve whispered and climbed down to the ground.

Andrew did the same and, once he was sure they were alone, said, "What is this place? Am I dreaming?"

"If you're dreaming, then I'm dreaming, too," she said.

"Not unless you're just saying that in my dream," he countered.

"We need to get dressed," she said.

"Get dressed? For what?"

"You don't want anyone to see you like that." She took a few steps and Andrew realized they were back at the ivy curtain and the cave. Reaching behind some bushes nearby, Eve pulled out a sack. "I hope these fit. I grabbed them along the way."

"Along the way?" he asked.

She pulled clothes out of the sack and handed them to him. "Put those on."

Before he could say anything, she disappeared behind another thick bush.

"Are we part of the show?" he asked as he looked at the clothes she'd given him. They were made of a rough fabric.

"Hurry, before someone sees you," she called out. "The clothes will feel itchy at first."

Andrew had to make a decision. Was he playing along or putting an end to this craziness? What if he refused? What would happen if he dashed back into the cave to go home? Would he see the clock pendulum and the light from the room of clocks?

He pushed the ivy aside. A wall of stone faced him. The cave was gone.

"You can't get back like that," Eve said from behind the bush. "Now, get dressed."

Andrew changed into the clothes Eve had given him. He pulled on a green shirt that felt like it was made of leather. It came down to the middle of his thighs. It was rough and uncomfortable. Next came thick brown leggings, probably wool and definitely itchy. They fit his legs like a tight pair of jeans, but hung loose around his waist. A belt fixed that. It was made of interwoven strips of leather. There was no buckle, so Andrew had to tie it in the front. He sat on the ground to yank on a pair of dark brown leather boots. They covered his feet with room to spare and went up to his knees.

Eve emerged from behind the bush. She wore a brown tunic, probably wool, that reached down to her knees. A thin strap cinched it around her waist. A vest of leather hung over the tunic. Green leggings covered her legs. Leather shoes reached just above her ankles.

She nodded to him, then gathered up their clothes and shoved them into the sack. She hid it behind the bush again.

"Come on," she said. She picked up a satchel and slung it over her shoulder. She strode into the forest.

"To where?" Andrew asked, following her yet again. He stumbled over fallen branches. He groaned. "Don't they have hiking trails here?"

"Just watch where you're going," Eve said. "You'll get used to it."

"Used to what?" he demanded. "Where are we? Where are we going?"

"*There*," Eve said and pointed.

Through the trees, Andrew saw a mansion with big gray stones, tall windows, and chimneys sticking out here and there. It was like something out of an old movie.

He picked up his pace, now running through the woods toward the mansion, stumbling more.

They reached the edge of the forest. A field stretched out between them and the mansion.

The field is real, he thought. *The mansion is real.* He didn't know what to do with all the things his eyes and ears and sense of touch were telling him was true. He felt a growing sense of panic. His mind kept saying, *This can't be happening. It's impossible.*

Eve touched his arm.

He jerked away from her. "Have I gone crazy?" he asked. "Did I take the wrong allergy medicine this morning?"

She gave him a coy smile and those funny-colored eyes of hers seemed to sparkle. "I asked if you were serious."

"But you didn't say anything about *this*," he said.

"It'll make sense as you go along," Eve said. "Just stay close to me."

"You've done this before?" he asked.

She nodded and said firmly, "Do what I say and you'll be okay." She looked around and signaled for him to follow her as she picked up her speed for the mansion. She ran like a graceful animal, leaping over the pits and potholes that threatened to trip Andrew.

They reached a high stone wall that led to a wooden gate. They went through to a stony courtyard. A ramshackle stable made of rocks and wood sat on the opposite side.

The servants Andrew had seen in the forest were now in the middle of the courtyard, their eyes focused on their task to skin the boar. Andrew paused to look at the mess of fur and muscle and bone until Eve tugged at his sleeve.

They crept along the wall to an arched opening. A passage led between two walls to an open gate. Eve stopped.

The silver-haired man and the two younger ones from the forest were sitting at a table in the center of another courtyard. Servants moved around them with plates and pitchers.

Andrew's mind raced with questions. *A lot* of questions. Apart from anything to do with where they were, he wanted to know who these people were and why they had followed them here. *Surely this is trespassing*, he thought.

He put his hand on Eve's shoulder and was about to ask, but someone shouted, "My Lord, the Lady Anne is here to see you!"

"This is what I came to see," Eve said over her shoulder, as if she knew Andrew's question.

With the announcement about Lady Anne, the three men at the table looked at each other. The clean-shaven younger man smirked. The bearded one sneered.

The older man waved at the servant and said, "Bid her enter."

The servant disappeared through a door and returned seconds later with a woman wearing a long dark dress—or it might have been a coat; Andrew wasn't sure. Her long brown hair was adorned with a purple headdress, held in place by a gold ringlet. She looked young and walked confidently to the table.

The men stood up. The older man gave a terse bow. "You are a vision of loveliness," he said.

Lady Anne curtsied to him, "You are too kind, Sir Reynauld." She gave an obligatory curtsy to the two young men. "My lord Maurice," she said to the one with the beard. "My lord Everard," she said to the one without.

The two young men bowed to her.

"Sit, my lady," Sir Reynauld said. "Refresh yourself with us."

Lady Anne shook her head. "Forgive me, my lord, but I shall not. I come bearing news."

The men remained standing. Everard shifted uncomfortably.

"I have paid the ransom for my husband Bennett's release," Lady Anne announced.

"Have you?" Sir Reynauld asked with undisguised surprise.

"The treasure has been delivered to the castle of Cormac at Loch Earn. My husband will be returning."

"I am overjoyed to hear it," Sir Reynauld said, not sounding overjoyed at all.

"When do you expect your husband's arrival?" asked the young man called Maurice.

"Within a fortnight, my lord," she said. "I believe that will give you sufficient time to depart from our home."

Sir Reynauld and the two young men gave each other sideways glances.

"*Depart*, dear woman? Why would we do that?" Sir Reynauld asked.

Lady Anne looked stunned. "My lord, the estates of Havelond rightfully belong to my husband and his family. Our lord, the abbot, gave you possession of them merely as service to maintain the lands in my husband's absence."

"So we have," said Sir Reynauld. "We have worked diligently, sparing nothing."

"You have done well by my husband's misfortune and benefited from the abundance of our lands," she said quickly. "More so than ever you did at your home in Prestbury."

"I will not deny it, my lady," Sir Reynauld said, his voice silky smooth. "Your husband has been gone for *two years*. Such a long time! We might be forgiven to think of Havelond as our home."

"'Tis home, but not yours for the taking," Lady Anne said.

Sir Reynauld held up his hand. "By law, we are permitted—"

Lady Anne cut him off. "You will remember, Sir Reynauld, that my husband departed to fight for the king against the Scottish plunderers. He was taken captive in that effort."

Sir Reynauld nodded. "A noble effort with a tragic turn. And we have honored him by maintaining the lands in good faith, however—"

Lady Anne's tone sharpened. "In *good* faith? My lord, you drove me from my home and forced me to a cottage on the outskirts of our estate."

"Have you not been comfortable, my lady?" he asked. "How was I to know unless you told me?"

"Are you saying you received none of my messages?" Lady Anne asked.

Sir Reynauld looked insulted. "I have *not*, my lady. Be assured I shall have the servants beaten for their incompetence."

The servant by the door looked worried.

"Sir Reynauld," Lady Anne said, "upon my husband's return, he will reclaim what is rightfully his."

Sir Reynauld gave her a snake-like smile. "We shall discuss the matter when he does."

"So we shall. Good day, sir." Lady Anne gave him a stiff curtsy, turned on her heels, and strode across the courtyard.

"My lady!" Sir Reynauld called out. "Allow me to have my sons accompany you!"

"I would rather walk alone," she called back to him as she went through the door. The servant hustled after her.

Andrew had been watching the scene and was suddenly confused in a whole new way. Their English was not his English, he realized. And not just their accents. He'd seen enough movies and had even gone to a production of *Hamlet* in Denver. He knew how the British sounded. But the *words* he heard were different. They were from an older kind of English. They reminded him of a book a teacher had read to his class in sixth grade. Something *Tales* by Somebody Chaucer. He had struggled to keep up with that old English. What confused him now was that he *understood* what Lady Anne and Sir Reynauld and the others had been saying, as if they'd been speaking in a kind of English he recognized. *How?* He would have to add that question to all of the others.

Maurice said, "Surely we will not give up Havelond, Father."

Sir Reynauld sat down, and the other two did the same. He picked up a chalice. "In truth, the law sides with the Lady Anne and her husband Bennett. Upon his return, the lands belong with him. However . . ." His voice trailed off and he upended the silver chalice into his mouth.

Everard said, "*However?*"

"If something befell him on the road from Scotland . . . then our circumstances would most-assuredly change." Sir Reynauld slowly shook his head. "How sad it is that, in these times, a man may not be safe from robbers and unscrupulous men."

Maurice suddenly stood up. "Come along, brother."

Everard looked puzzled. "Are we going somewhere?"

"Let us hope to find our lord Bennett along the road from Scotland, to give him protection," Maurice said. He grinned.

Everard smiled as he also stood. "Yes. I see."

Maurice and Everard bowed to their father and marched to the door. A moment later, servants brought Sir Reynauld plates covered with food. Andrew thought he saw vegetables and various small animals.

He turned to Eve, but she was backing away, gesturing for him to retreat down the passage. He began to turn, when he bumped into something big and solid. A heavy hand fell on his shoulder. Another grabbed Eve.

"Now you are in for it," said a low growl.

3

A gigantic man with the face of a potato and a thick black beard dragged Andrew and Eve back to the stable courtyard.

"I have warned you beggars to keep out," he said. He tossed them to the ground.

The other servants lifted their heads, turning their attention from the boar.

"A beating will teach you," the man said and snatched a horse whip from a hook just inside the stable.

"Please, sir," Eve said. "We did not come to beg."

"You shouldn't be here at all." He raised the whip.

Andrew crawled between Eve and the bearded man, ready to take the blow.

Another voice shouted, "Stay your hand!"

The bearded man scowled.

A man emerged from the stable. It was the head servant from the forest. "Are you mad?" he cried out. "Why are you dealing with beggars when you must light the fire for the pit? The master is waiting! Their beating will be nothing compared to *your* beating if we're delayed."

The bearded man snarled, then kicked at Andrew. "Out," he said.

Andrew scrambled to his feet, pulling at Eve's arm.

The man waved the whip at them as Andrew half-pulled Eve through the gate and back to the field beyond.

"Will you *please* tell me what is going on," Andrew said.

"There's no time," Eve said and darted off, running along the wall.

Andrew chased after her. "Where are we going?" he asked. "The woods are *that* way!"

"We have to follow the Lady Anne," Eve called back to him.

"*Why?*" Andrew asked.

"She needs our help," she said and sprinted away from him.

It was all Andrew could do to keep up. They followed the wall to the front gate of the mansion and a road that cut through the forest ahead of them.

Eve slowed to a fast walk. "There she is," Eve said.

Lady Anne walked with her head down and shoulders slumped. As they approached from behind, she suddenly whirled around, as if she thought she was about to be attacked. She then relaxed when she saw the two kids.

"I beg your forgiveness, children," she said. Her eyes were red, as if she'd been crying. "I have no purse, nor money to give."

"We are not beggars, my lady," Eve said. "Master Robin has sent me to you."

Lady Anne's eyes widened. "My dear cousin Robin?" She glanced back at the mansion nervously, then said, "Come. We must not speak in the open."

They followed the road until it came to a narrow path. The path took them a short distance to a cottage made of dark stone and a roof made of branches, twigs, and leaves. The front entrance was arched, with a door made of one piece of solid wood.

Lady Anne lifted the latch and pushed open the door. She stepped in, looking around to make sure no one was there. She waved them in and closed the door.

The inside of the cottage was all one room. A fireplace took up one wall, with black pots and pans and long utensils hanging from its mantelpiece. Fat wooden beams held up the roof. A small bird flitted in the rafters. The floor was made of uneven slabs of stone.

A round polished table and four chairs sat in the center of the room, a vase and flowers placed on top. Nearby stood a hutch with two shelves of plates and cups as its upper half, and a cabinet with drawers comprising its lower half. A smaller chest with drawers sat next to it.

In one corner of the cottage was a bed with a carved headboard and matching frame and footboard. A thick homemade quilt covered a thin mattress. A small stand holding a bowl and pitcher sat to the side. On the floor at the foot of the bed lay a small cot. In another corner stood a spinning wheel and a wooden box of raw wool.

It was a warm day and the cottage was hot and stuffy. The smell of wood and dampness was oppressive. There were only two windows, and square holes with wooden shutters closed over them.

"I dare not leave the shutters open when I am away," Lady Anne said and quickly unlatched them. She pushed them open and a hint of fresh air wafted in. She bade them to sit down at the table while she took plates from the shelf of the hutch. "I have a servant," she said, "but she is at the market now."

She opened the doors of the cabinet and brought out plates of bread and cheese. Then came small wooden cups that she filled with water.

Lady Anne sat down at the table. Andrew noticed that she didn't have a plate. Still, she did the Sign of the Cross and said softly, "For these gifts and your many abundant blessings, we give thanks, O Lord."

Andrew and Eve made the Sign of the Cross.

"Please, eat," Lady Anne said.

The bread was hard and broke apart as Andrew picked it up. He put some in his mouth. It was dry and crumbly. He drank from the cup, just to wash it down. He nearly spat everything out as he coughed and gasped. "This is not water," he choked.

"'Tis ale," Lady Anne said. "Is it not to your liking?"

Andrew didn't want to be rude and said, "I was surprised."

Eve laughed at him. "Ale is often better for you than the water."

Andrew looked at Eve and all the questions he wanted to ask her came back to mind.

"What are your names?" Lady Eve asked.

"I am Evangeline," Eve said. "Though I am most often called Eve."

"I am Andrew."

"How long have you been in the service of my cousin Robin?" Lady Anne asked.

"A short time," said Eve.

"Since he became an outlaw?" Lady Anne asked.

"Aye," Eve said.

Lady Anne looked at them with eyes of sympathy. "I am saddened to think of what circumstances took you to him."

"I was lost and he found me," Eve said.

"And you?" Lady Anne asked Andrew.

"I am . . . new here," Andrew said.

"Please, then: tell me of my dear cousin," Lady Anne said to Eve.

"He sent me to see if you are well and in need of anything. He heard that your husband is finally returning home," Eve said.

Lady Anne's eyes filled with tears. "Robin is so kind," she said. She pulled a handkerchief from her sleeve and dabbed at her eyes.

"You are having trouble with the men in the mansion," Eve said.

Lady Anne gave a deep sigh. "'Tis a sorrowful business," she said. "My husband Bennett fought for King Henry against usurpers in Scotland. He was captured and has been held for ransom these past two years. The abbot, who owns these lands, allowed Sir Reynauld and his sons to care for the house and fields in my husband's absence. I believed it was an act of mercy. Then their carousing and decadent living caused me great fear. I left my house and came to our gamekeeper's cottage. Here I have been while I raised the money for my husband's ransom. By the grace of God, it has been paid and he will return."

"Do you believe Sir Reynauld will depart?" Eve said.

Lady Anne shook her head.

"I will tell Master Robin of your plight," Eve said firmly. "He will come to your aid."

Lady Anne put her face in her hands and sobbed. "I know he will. Yet I fear for him. Sir Reynauld is befriended by evil and corrupt men."

Eve stood up and said to Andrew, "We must go now, if we're to reach him before dark."

Andrew choked down a piece of bread and rose to his feet.

Lady Anne rose. "You must take the bread and cheese for your journey." She took two large rags from the hutch and wrapped up the food.

Eve put the food inside her satchel and bowed. "Thank you, my lady."

"May God give you strength and speed," she said.

Andrew bowed too and said, "Be of good cheer," because he'd heard it in a school play once and it seemed like the right thing to say.

Out in the sunshine again, Lady Anne stood in the doorway, weeping and waving to them until the path took them out of sight. They came onto the main road. Eve quickened her step.

This time, Andrew moved faster, getting a few steps in front of her. Then he turned and stopped. Eve nearly ran into him.

"What is wrong?" she asked.

"*What is wrong?*" Andrew asked. "I don't know where we are or how we got here or what we're doing here or if any of this is even real, and you ask, '*What is wrong?*'"

She frowned and pushed past him. "Keep up and I will try to explain. We have to get this news to Master Robin."

"Let's start there," Andrew said, staying by her side. "Who is Master Robin?"

"Robert of Locksley," she said.

"I've heard that name," Andrew said, but he couldn't remember from where.

"You know him as Robin Hood," Eve said.

Andrew stopped again. "Robin Hood? *The* Robin Hood? The steals-from-the-rich-to-give-to-the-poor Robin Hood?"

"That's all wrong," Eve said, walking backward to coax him along. "He doesn't steal from the rich. Some of his best friends are rich. He takes from those who have harmed others by cheating or stealing or . . . worse."

She turned and walked on.

Andrew was stunned. "But Robin Hood isn't real," he said, catching up again.

"You should say that to him when you meet him," she said, giving him a wry look.

"How do you know him?" Andrew asked.

"Like I said to Lady Anne, I was lost and he found me."

"You were lost? *Here?*"

"It was my first trip back," she said.

"Your first? How many trips have you taken?" Andrew asked, not even sure what he meant by the word "trip."

"A few," she said. "And I was like you. Completely confused."

"Confused is hardly the word for it," Andrew said, then pleaded, "*Please* tell me all the things you aren't telling me!"

A sideways glance and a small smile came to Eve's face. "It's going to be hard for you to believe."

"It can't be harder than this," he said, spreading his arms. "I'm walking on a dirt road that you say is in the time of Robin Hood. How hard can the rest of it be?"

She looked at him, the unusual color of her eyes alight. "You'll find out."

"Explain it to me," he insisted.

And she did.

This is what Eve told him.

Once upon a time, back in the early part of the twentieth century, there was a respectable and successful businessman named Alfred Virtue. Everyone in Hope Springs knew him. He was likable when it came to people and shrewd when it came to money. He served on the city council and established a profitable bank and invested in all kinds of businesses like railroads, mines, and property.

More than making money, Alfred Virtue loved adventure and exploration. He often ventured off to places like Europe and Africa. He journeyed to the northern reaches of Canada and the southern-most parts of South America. Some said he had sailed to both the North and South Poles.

"It was the time of the great explorers," Eve explained. "Writers marveled at the vast unknown parts of the earth. Jules Verne, H. G. Wells, Arthur Conan Doyle, and Edgar Rice Burroughs told stories of lost worlds and ancient civilizations. People were discovering the world in a whole new way."

During his many travels, Alfred Virtue had heard about the "Radiant Stone." Some said the stone was like a black diamond; others described it as being red or green, with the facets of a diamond or some other precious gem. The Radiant Stone was called by different names in different parts of the world, and historical accounts and archaeological findings put the stone in different times. The myths claimed the stone had magical, even fearsome, powers. Stories told of people who touched the stone and disappeared forever. Others touched it, disappeared, but came back babbling like the insane about the impossible things they'd seen.

At first, Alfred Virtue thought they were merely legends, like the lost city of Atlantis, the Fountain of Youth, or the Loch Ness monster. But the more he heard the stories about the stone, the more he began to believe that there was an element of truth to them.

Eventually, Alfred Virtue concluded there wasn't just one Radiant Stone, but many of them scattered all over the world. They were found in caves and forests, on mountainsides and in riverbeds.

Alfred Virtue slowly collected the legends and the stories, and dared to hope he might find one of the stones on one of his many expeditions. Then, during a trip to Ireland, he met an old man at a pub who professed an intimate knowledge of the Radiant Stone. The old man told how the ancient Druids had found one and thought its power and magic came from the goddess Arianrhod, the "Keeper of the Circling Wheel of Silver" in the sky. She had the power of time and reincarnation and "sky-weaving enchantments." The Druids put the stone in an idol dedicated to her and worshiped it for years.

The arrival of Saint Patrick and Christianity to Ireland changed everything. The old gods were chased out as the people committed themselves to Jesus Christ. The idols were put aside or destroyed. A Druid priest hid the idol with the Radiant Stone in a labyrinth of caves. But a Christian named Aeric, nicknamed the "God Hunter" because he dedicated himself to hunting the idols, found where the Druids had hidden the Radiant Stone. A battle ensued. Aeric was killed, but a young Christian named Brendon escaped with the stone and delivered it to Saint Brigid. Brigid later carried the stone to the Beckery Chapel in Glastonbury, England. Glastonbury was famous for its stories about King Arthur, and that's where Alfred Virtue eventually recovered it.

Alfred Virtue brought the stone back to Hope Springs for examination. It was then he discovered what the stone *really* did.

"And what was that?" Andrew asked.

They were now deep in the middle of a forest somewhere. Birds called out far away. The buzzing of the many bugs had faded off. It seemed like his voice was the only sound for miles around, the thick gathering of leaves overhead and bed of detritus underfoot muting the world.

Andrew asked, "Well? What did Alfred Virtue discover?"

"Time travel," Eve said. She reached up to her neck and pulled at the silver chain. She lifted it over her head and revealed something that looked like a large medallion.

She held it out and Andrew thought it actually looked more like an oversized pocket watch, with a silver cover and a stem on the top. "That's the Radiant Stone?" Andrew asked.

"That's the case," she said. "It needs one to keep anyone from touching the stone by accident." She held the case in her palm with her fingers around one side and her thumb on the stem at the top. She pressed down on the stem. The silver cover sprung open on a little hinge.

"This is the Radiant Stone," she said with a hint of pride.

Andrew expected to see the face of a clock. Instead, the inside was filled with a shiny jewel. It was covered with a lot of facets that caught the light in different ways, sometimes looking green or red or blue, even black.

"What happens if I touch it?" Andrew asked, lifting his finger as if he might.

Eve pulled her hand back to make sure he didn't. "You'll go to another time." She presented it again. "All those facets are different points in time. If you touch one with the tip of your finger, you'll go there."

Andrew put his hands behind his back and looked closely. Some of the facets were bigger than others. "Which one did you touch to get here?"

She carefully pointed to a green facet near the lower left-hand side of the stone. "That one."

"Why that one?"

She shrugged. "I don't know. All I know is that Alfred Virtue drew a diagram of the whole stone. It shows every facet and where it takes you if you touch it. He tested them all."

"He went back to all those different times?" Andrew asked, amazed. "There are dozens of facets."

"Even more on the back," she said.

Andrew tried to imagine Alfred Virtue touching a facet, going back in time, then returning to the present to make notes. "It must have taken him ages to figure them all out."

"It didn't take any time at all," Eve said. "While we're here, no time is passing for us back home. And when we're back home, no time is passing here."

"Time *stops*?" Andrew asked.

She shook her head. "It's hard to explain. Time is moving, but the stone lets us step *out* of it. And then, if we go back, we enter the same point we left. Like a book mark, I guess. The story doesn't really stop because you put it aside. There are a lot of pages left. It only seems to stop because you came away from it."

Andrew rubbed his forehead. This felt like figuring out a really hard math problem. "So, right now your aunt is in the shop and she has no idea we've been gone for hours? And when we walk out of that room of clocks again, it'll be like we had just walked into it?"

Eve nodded again. "I left here over a week ago, according to our time. I went to see Lady Anne, like Master Robin told me, but I had to leave. It was a week for me, but no time here."

"Why did you have to leave?"

"Homework," Eve said.

Andrew laughed.

She snapped the cover closed.

"Is it heavy?" Andrew asked.

She handed him the case. It wasn't heavy at all. In fact, he was surprised by how light it was.

He handed the case back to her. She slipped the silver chain over her head and dropped the case under her tunic.

As they walked on in silence, Andrew's mind was spinning. If she had told him all of this back at the shop, he wouldn't have believed her. But there was nothing left to doubt. They were *here*, not in the shop. That thought led Andrew to another important question. He asked, "How do we get back to our time?"

"It's simple," she said. "You just press your hand on the entire stone and it takes you back to where you belong. I guess touching all of the facets at the same time is like a reset button."

"Wait a minute," he said. "I never touched the stone. How did I get here?"

"I held your hand," she said. "It worked through me to you."

They climbed over a fallen tree, worked their way around a thick section of bushes, and emerged from the dense woods onto a narrow path. It was getting late in the afternoon. Andrew realized his legs were aching. He had no idea how long they'd been walking, or if they were anywhere near where they were supposed to be.

Eve suddenly put a hand up to stop.

"What's wrong?" he asked.

"Hide," she said and pushed him back into the bushes.

They crouched down. Andrew peered through the tangle of branches, beyond the path to the woods on the other side. A young girl came into view—he guessed she was seven or eight, the age of his little sister Sam. She had dark unkempt hair and wore a long coat with a hood. Hanging from her hand was a small sack. She walked as if she was searching for something. She came to the path, paused to look around, then crossed in their direction.

The girl stopped at their hiding place and began to pluck berries, putting them into the sack. Andrew saw tears falling down her face, making dull white lines through her dirty cheeks, but she made no sound. Her face was thin, her lips were drawn in, and her eyes looked big against the dark circles underneath them. She reminded him of pictures he'd seen of starving kids in foreign countries. She used her free hand to rub at her runny nose. He noticed her hands were scratched, the skin on her fingers split. Her coat was torn in places.

She was only a couple of feet away. Her gaze was fixed on the berries in front of her, but Andrew could imagine her alarm if she suddenly saw them. *Do we stay hidden or let her know we're here?* he hoped his expression asked Eve.

Eve answered by standing up. "Greetings!" she said.

The girl jumped and stumbled back.

"Do not be afraid," Eve said as calmly as she could. She slowly stepped out onto the path.

The girl jerked her head to the left and right. She was checking her options to run.

"We will not harm you," Eve said, raising her hands. She gestured for Andrew to stand up.

When he did, the girl let out a little screech and dashed across the path to the woods.

They both watched the girl run away. She tripped, clambered to her feet, and raced onward, looking back to make sure they weren't following her.

"Do you think she's lost?" Andrew asked. "Maybe she needs help."

"We don't have time to find out," Eve said.

"What if she's in trouble?"

"We have to deliver our message to Master Robin," she said. "Someone else will find her." She turned and started down the path.

"Who?" he asked impatiently. "There's no one else out here. We can't abandon a young girl."

"She'll be found," Eve said firmly.

He was about to argue with her when they heard a terrified scream.

Andrew and Eve rushed through the woods toward the sound of the scream. It was the girl, Andrew had no doubt, but he couldn't imagine why she was screaming. *Do they have bears here?* he wondered.

Up ahead he saw a man with his back to them. He was dressed in the rough clothes Andrew had seen on the servants at the mansion: a brown tunic with a belt made of rope and pants made of the same material as the tunic, but with patches sewn to it. A large knife was tucked in a sheath in his belt on the right side. A pouch hung from the belt on the left. He had hold of one of the girl's wrists.

She struggled to free herself.

The man said something to her, but she squirmed all the more and screeched at him.

Eve darted behind a tree and pulled at Andrew's arm to follow.

Andrew pulled away. He wasn't going to stand by while the girl was being hurt. He said so to Eve in the form of a grunt and grabbed the first stick he could find. *I'll sneak up on him*, he thought and tried to tiptoe in their direction.

As he drew closer, the girl saw him. Her expression betrayed that he was coming.

Still clutching the girl's arm, the man spun around. He had a rugged face with deep lines around his eyes and on his forehead. His chin was covered with stubble. "What is this?" he asked.

"Leave her alone!" Andrew shouted and raised his weapon.

The man looked at the stick. "What are you going to do with that, tickle me?"

"It is all right," Eve called out from behind Andrew. "God be with you, Master Will Scarlet!"

Will Scarlet? Andrew thought, remembering the name from the Robin Hood stories.

The man's eyes went from Andrew to Eve. He smiled and held up his free hand. "Hail, Waif of the Woods!"

Waif of the Woods?

Eve strode passed Andrew, whispering out of the corner of her mouth, "Get rid of the stick."

He threw down the stick and followed her.

"Please tell this child I will not harm her," Will Scarlet said to Eve.

The girl was pulling at her arm and attempted a few kicks at him.

"She might believe it if you will let go of her wrist," Eve suggested.

Will Scarlet frowned. "If I let her go, she will run. You know Master Robin will not suffer to have children alone in the forest."

Eve stepped close to the girl, who was wild-eyed from fear. "Listen to me," Eve said softly. "We can help you, if you will tell us who you are and why you are here."

The girl kept her eyes on Eve and slowly stopped struggling.

"What is your name?" Eve asked her.

"Ruth," the girl said.

"Do you promise not to run if he releases you?" Eve asked.

The girl looked unsure, looking at Eve, then Will Scarlet. She nodded.

Eve nodded to Will Scarlet. He reluctantly released his grip.

The girl didn't run. She looked at him unhappily and rubbed her wrist.

"Where are your parents?" Eve asked. "Are they hurt somewhere? Hungry? You were picking berries…"

"Hear me, little lass," Will Scarlet said. He knelt down next to the girl. She backed away. "There is not a village nor house anywhere nearby. From the tears in your cloak and the wear of your boots, you are either lost or you are running from someone or perhaps both. Is that so?"

The girl nodded.

"You are in good company," Will Scarlet said. "Have you heard of the outlaw Robin Hood?"

The girl's face brightened. "We are searching for him," she said.

We, Andrew thought.

Will Scarlet smiled. "You are closer to finding him than you know. Take us to your kin and, together, we will go to Master Robin. We have better food than berries and enough for all."

Her face betrayed her uncertainty. Andrew imagined her parents had told her not to reveal wherever they were hiding.

Her eyes locked on Andrew's.

He gave her an encouraging smile and a nod.

She let out a deep breath. "This way," she said.

Ruth led them through the forest and, eventually, to almost impassable growth of bushes. She easily slid beneath and through them. Eve, Will Scarlet, and Andrew pushed through, coming to a cliff at the edge of a ravine. A stream trickled at least twenty feet below. Ruth gave every appearance of stepping over the edge.

"Ruth?" Will Scarlet called out. The three of them rushed to the precipice and only then saw a path, hidden by the angle and sloping down to a ledge. Ruth stood waiting for them and then disappeared again.

One at a time, the three carefully walked down the slim path and came to a cave, obscured by the thicket. The girl was already inside. Andrew could hear her speaking in soft tones.

The three of them entered the cavity. The daylight, filtered by the thicket, cast a gray shadow. Andrew's eyes slowly adjusted, and he saw Ruth kneeling next to an old man lying on a makeshift bed of leaves. He was bundled in a coat that might have once been worn by a wealthy man but was now ragged and filthy. A large satchel sat nearby. Andrew noticed the blackened remains of a fire in a small circle of rocks nearby.

Ruth trembled as she glanced from the three to her father and back again. Even now, she looked afraid they might hurt them.

The old man slowly sat up, looking at them with watchful eyes. "Who is this? Ruth, are we betrayed?"

"Have no fear, master," said Will, bending down on one knee. "Your daughter has brought you aid." He drew the pouch from his belt and presented some slices of bread and meat to the old man. He gave some to Ruth.

The girl drew a small knife from the satchel and began to cut up the portions.

"There is enough for both of you," Will assured her.

The old man cried as he nibbled on the bread. "We have not eaten for three days," he said.

"Then you must eat slowly," Will Scarlet said.

"I thank you, good woodman," the old man said in a low quivering voice. The tears continued to fall. "It is not for myself that I am afraid, but in my present state, I am sure I have not long to live. I suffer anguish to think of my daughter left desolate."

"She will not be left desolate, nor shall I allow you to die," Will said. He grabbed a leather flask from another part of his belt. "Ale," he said.

The old man and his daughter drank, and a new light came into their eyes. Color returned to their cheeks.

With the help of his daughter, the old man crawled onto his knees. "Pray with me," he said and, without waiting, said, "O God of power and might, I give thanks to you for having delivered us from our misery…" He began to cry again. Ruth drew close and cried with him.

Eve and Andrew looked at each other. Andrew wondered what had happened to these poor people.

Will cleared his throat loudly and said in a gruff voice, "Are you able to travel?"

"I fear I am too weak from my illness. But I beg you to take my daughter to safety," the old man replied.

"You will both have safety," Will said. "Leave it to me."

The old man reached out and took Will's hand. "Hear me, good fellow. I am Reuben of Stamford, a Jew of York, and I pledge that if you will get me to my kinsmen in Nottingham, you will have the gratitude of me and my people forever, and our aid wherever you desire it."

"You offer more than I would ever ask," said Will. "What aid I may give you is not for your gratitude or your gold, but because it is always in my heart to help those in trouble."

The old man's eyes filled with new tears.

"Bide here until we return," Will said and gestured for Eve and Andrew to come out of the cave with him. They made their way up to the top of the cliff.

"I shall have a few words to say to Dodd about this," Will Scarlet grumbled when they were out of earshot. "'Tis his job to keep watch over this part of the forest. How does he not know about this man and girl?"

Eve gave a wry smile. "Dodd is known for his good heart, not his brains," she said.

Will chuckled. He gave Andrew a close look. "Who are you?"

"Andrew."

"Well, Andrew," he said. "Are you good with a staff, a bow, or a blade?"

Andrew stammered, "I am good with a bat and ball."

Will frowned and said, "Nevertheless, I have a task for you and our good waif Evangeline. Fly you both with all speed to Master Robin. Tell him of our need here. He will give his command about what to do."

For the next hour they ran. Eve bounded like a deer, but Andrew stumbled and tripped and could think of little else than the stitch in his side and how tired he felt.

They came to a part of the forest that looked as it probably had when prehistoric cave people walked through. *If they or anyone had ever walked through it*, Andrew thought.

"Are you sure we're going the right way?" he gasped.

Eve said, "Aye," and darted through a cluster of trees. Andrew was only a few steps behind her. They entered a

clearing and Andrew stopped. Men, dressed much like Will
Scarlet, sat on the grass or leaned against the trunks of trees;
a few were at roughly made tables and benches, eating from
wooden plates and bowls, or drinking from wooden cups.

"The Men of the Greenwood," Eve said to Andrew.

The men glanced at them with a cursory grunt or
nod. A couple of them greeted her—again calling her
"the waif." They came to a magnificent oak tree. More
men sat in a circle under its broad branches. They
looked as if they were in a serious business meeting,
talking in low and earnest voices. One of the assembly
saw Eve and signaled to a fellow sitting next to him,
who stood up and turned to them. This man had a
tanned, handsome, and honest face with lively, sharp
eyes and a broad, open smile. Dark brown curls adorned
his head. He was dressed in a tunic made of a rough
green cloth. Around his waist was a broad leather belt
with a sheath holding a dagger. He wore short breeches
of leather and leggings of green wool that reached
down to his ankles. His shoes were also made of a dark
brown leather.

"Master Robin," Eve said with a gentle bow.

"Evangeline! Our dear Waif of the Woods!" he
shouted happily. "I have been awaiting your return from
Havelond. How is my dear cousin Anne? Were you
forced to endure her bread-making skills?" He laughed

and turned his gaze to Andrew. "What is this, pray tell? You have found a boy?" he asked.

"His name is Andrew," Eve said.

"You are most welcome, Andrew," Robin said with a courteous bow and wave of his hand.

Robin Hood, Andrew thought, his mind seizing up. *I am meeting Robin Hood—live and in person!*

"Th—tha—thank you, good sir," Andrew stammered and blushed.

"Master, we have two urgent matters," Eve said. She told him about the Lady Anne and her problems with Sir Reynauld, then continued with their encounter with Reuben of Stamford and his daughter Ruth.

Robin swung around to the men in the circle. "Good fellows! On your feet!"

The men were up in an instant. One, a giant of a man, rose above the rest and asked, "What is it, Master Robin?"

"Little John," Robin said to the giant, "take a few men with you and spread out to the main roads leading to Scotland. Search them for my cousin's husband, Bennett of Havelond. See that he is conducted safely to me."

Little John! Andrew thought.

Eve nudged him and whispered, "You're not going to faint, are you?"

"That is Little John," Andrew whispered back.

Robin added, "Oh—and send Hob o' the Hill to my cousin's cottage to make sure she is protected. I do not trust Sir Reynauld nor his sons to leave her undisturbed."

"Aye, Master," said Little John and he strode off with big lumbering steps.

"Someone find Dodd for me," Robin called out.

Andrew could hear voices calling Dodd's name echoing throughout the camp.

A few minutes later, a very round man came bustling up, pulling at his breeches as if they might fall down. "You summoned me, Master Robin?"

"That is Dodd, son of Alstan," Eve whispered to Andrew.

Robin gave him a stern look. "Dodd, why have I received a message from Will Scarlet about an old man and his daughter living in a cave in Barrow Down? 'Tis your area to watch, is it not?"

Dodd turned red-faced and said, "An old man and his daughter? In Barrow Down?"

"They have been there for a few days." Robin's face lost its amiability.

Dodd stammered, but said nothing helpful.

Robin frowned. "Take Nigel and anyone else you need, along with two horses. Carry the old man and his daughter to the Huntsman's Lodge. You know where it is? You will not lose your way?"

"Aye, Master Robin," Dodd said. "I mean, *no*, Master Robin."

"See to it, Dodd. I will not countenance any excuses," he added.

"No, Master Robin. That is to say, yes, Master Robin. I mean—"

"*Go!*" Robin commanded.

Dodd rushed off, still pulling at his breeches.

Andrew turned to Robin again. The outlaw was looking at him with a curious expression.

"From what village do you hail?" he asked.

"Hope Springs," Andrew replied.

He looked puzzled. "I know it not."

"'Tis far from here," Eve said.

Robin kept his eyes on Andrew. "I feel as though I have met someone who looks very much like you, though older. Your father, perhaps?"

"My father has never been here," Andrew said.

"Another relative perhaps," Robin said, dismissing the subject.

"Perhaps," Andrew repeated, unsure of who Robin was thinking of.

Robin put one hand on Andrew's shoulder and the other on Eve's. "Eat now. Rest well this night. By God's grace, we will go to the Huntsman's Lodge tomorrow to see about our mysterious cave dwellers."

"Thank you, Master Robin," Eve said.

As the two walked away, Eve whispered to Andrew, "Theodore Perry."

"What about him?" Andrew asked.

"He was best friends with Alfred Virtue," she said. "You look like him."

"So?"

"I think he's been here. That is why Robin thinks you look familiar."

Andrew was stunned. "My great-great-*whatever* traveled through time? He met Robin Hood?"

Eve was amused. "Why are you so surprised? Alfred Virtue trusted Theodore Perry more than anyone. Why not let him take a trip to the past?"

Andrew shook his head. *What else am I going to learn about the Radiant Stone and my family?* he wondered.

Eve led him to a campfire where a short, elf-like man named Arthur a Bland ladled stew from a large black cauldron. He was happy to see "the Waif."

The stew had big chunks of meat and potatoes and a green vegetable that might have been cabbage. Andrew wasn't sure.

"The meat is venison," Eve said. "If we came earlier, we would have had venison pies, some fish, roast duck, and partridges."

Andrew was given a big portion of bread that was easier to chew than the Lady Anne's version. Dunking it in the stew made it even better. The meat was chewy and had a tangy taste.

Darkness fell and Eve showed Andrew to a tree under which someone had made a bed of leaves. "This is where Dodd usually sleeps. He won't be back tonight. It's yours."

"Where will you be?" Andrew asked.

She pointed to another tree a couple of yards away.

"Do they have wild animals here?" Andrew asked. "I won't be attacked by a boar, will I?"

She smiled. "There aren't a lot of boars in England now. The boar you saw this morning was probably brought in from France by Sir Reynauld. The rich can afford them, to hunt for sport."

"No wonder the boar was so unhappy." Andrew stretched out on the bed. It felt the way he expected a mattress of leaves to feel. "I won't be able to sleep," he said, thinking how his day had started with a normal breakfast at home and ended with him in the camp of Robin Hood.

Eve said good night and went to her tree.

Andrew tossed and turned, tossed and turned again, found a comfortable position, and kept thinking, *What a strange day*, when he fell into a deep sleep.

Something was nudging Andrew's foot. Then he felt a tug at the tip of his boot.

"Stop it," he said, thinking his brother Nick was messing around.

More nudging and tugging.

He groaned and rolled over to see a deer trying to eat his foot.

He shouted, pulling his legs away as he sat up. The deer gave him a dull look.

Andrew hugged his knees as it all came back to him: The woods. Robin Hood. *Time travel.*

Eve was sitting up in her makeshift bed. "Don't mind him. That's Rodric. He wandered in one day as if no one would even *think* to eat him for dinner. Everyone says he's got sawdust for brains."

Andrew shook his head. "Maybe he does if he thinks my foot is food."

Seeing that the foot would not be returned, Rodric wandered off.

"How did you sleep?" Eve asked.

Andrew moved his head back and forth and up and down. His neck ached. He realized he'd used a fat tree root as a pillow.

Robin's men were up and moving this way and that as if they had important things to do.

"Let's go down to the pond and wash," Eve said.

They traversed the camp, passing some men practicing with swords, others with long staffs. Andrew heard rustling in the trees overhead and saw a few men leaping from branch to branch. One misjudged the distance and fell to the ground with a painful thud. A short distance away, archers shot arrows from longbows at something Andrew couldn't see.

"Robin makes them practice a lot," Eve said.

They walked down a grassy hill to a large pond. Arthur a Bland and a young man were filling pitchers with water.

Eve and Andrew knelt on the bank. She splashed water on her head, face, and neck. Andrew leaned forward to do the same and saw a fish darting away under the surface.

There was a big splash on the far side of the pond. Andrew looked up to see a man swimming. He hoped the man was dressed.

After trying to scrub himself with the cool water, Andrew lay back on the soft grass to let the morning sun dry his face. "I dreamt about traveling through time," he said to Eve. "But the dream was a jumble of Lady Anne's cottage and the long walk through the woods and the little girl picking berries. And I think I saw a man standing somewhere in the forest who might have been Theodore Perry. He was watching me."

"Alfred Virtue wrote about the effect time travel has on our minds," Eve said softly, looking around to make sure no one was listening. "He wondered if it might drive a person crazy."

Andrew said, "Right now, I'm going crazy wondering how a stone can let us travel through time. How does it work?"

"That is the mystery," Eve said. "Alfred Virtue had a theory that the Radiant Stone somehow absorbs time and makes time part of itself. Then it becomes a gateway back to the time it has absorbed."

Andrew considered the idea. "You mean, it'd be like a computer camera capturing images and putting them on a hard drive and then letting you enter into the images?"

Eve shrugged.

"But how can a *stone* record time?" Andrew asked.

"How does anything in nature do what it does? I'm not a scientist. I really don't know. Alfred Virtue didn't know either. He had all kinds of theories, but none he thought was the answer."

"Can the stone send us *anywhere* in time?" Andrew asked.

"Do you mean, to any time or any location in time?"

"Both."

"Alfred Virtue said a Radiant Stone picks up history in the area where it is located." She put a hand to her tunic and Andrew knew she was touching the case underneath.

"*This* stone can take us to points of history in Ireland and England or wherever it's been. Even Hope Springs, I guess, because Alfred Virtue took it there. Other stones can take us to whatever places and points in history they picked up around them."

"So, a Radiant Stone in Rome would take us back to Roman history. One in Moscow would take us to Russian history…"

"That's the idea."

"Did Alfred ever figure out where the stones originally came from?"

Eve nudged at a pebble with her foot and said, "Maybe they came from a meteorite that hit the earth in prehistoric times."

"That wouldn't explain the stones being all over the world," Andrew said. "Unless it *rained* meteorites."

"Maybe they're the same meteorites that killed the dinosaurs," Eve suggested. "But Alfred also wondered if the Radiant Stones came from deep inside the earth itself."

"They worked themselves up through the crust?" Andrew asked.

Eve nodded.

"Then why aren't they lying all over the place?" Andrew countered. "Why doesn't everyone know about them?"

"They're not like diamonds or the kinds of gems people are looking for."

"Okay, but shouldn't there be more stories about people disappearing or showing up back in time, like us?"

Eve tucked her arms behind her head and lay back on the grass. She closed her eyes. "The stone doesn't work for everyone," she said.

"What do you mean?"

"I mean, there are some people who could pick one up and nothing would happen to them. Other people touch one and—*zoom*—they're gone."

"Why would it work for some and not for others?" Andrew asked.

"I don't know," Eve admitted. "Maybe it's like people who are allergic to some things and others aren't. Maybe it's a special combination of whatever the stone is made of and something about the person holding it. I really don't understand it. But it worked for me, and I knew it would work for you."

Andrew turned to her. "How did you know that?"

She pushed up onto her elbow and looked at him, her pale eyes shimmering. "Remember the first time you came into the store, before Christmas? I saw how you reacted to the place."

"It was an interesting store," Andrew said. "I like history. And I was surprised that it was connected to my family. It was a shock to find out that I look like Theodore Perry."

"It was more than all that," she said, coaxing him.

"Well, yeah. I guess I felt like—it's weird to say—but it was like the past came alive, just for a minute."

"That's what I saw in you," Eve said. "Your face looked like the way I felt the first time I came into the shop."

"Is that why you were watching me?" he asked. "Is that what the whole hide-and-seek thing was about?"

She smiled at him. "I see people come in and out of the shop all the time, and you are the only one who reacted like I did. Even Aunt Catherine doesn't get it."

Andrew thought about that. "Are you saying there is something inside of me that's connected to the stone, or something in the stone that's connected to me? Like a magnet?"

Eve sat up. "It's not just the stone. There is something about the Old Bank Building. Alfred Virtue built some strange things into it. You should see the basement when we get back."

He remembered that Catherine Drake had said something about the basement.

"Are you sure it's not some kind of magic?" Andrew asked. "Maybe we're messing around with . . . something evil."

Eve grimaced. "It isn't supernatural. I'm sure an expert could explain it all with wormholes or dark matter or things like that. Besides, Alfred Virtue wouldn't have messed with anything supernatural. He was a good Catholic. So was Theodore Perry."

Maybe we should show the stone to an expert," Andrew said.

"And have them take it away from me for tests? No way," she countered. "Somebody will want to turn it into a new kind of weapon. They always do in the movies."

A horn blew back at camp.

"We're late," Eve said and leapt to her feet.

Andrew stood up and, feeling his face go red, asked, "What do we do about . . . you know . . . going to the bathroom?"

Eve giggled. "Try behind that big tree to the left. Use the shovel."

Robin Hood assembled everyone for morning prayers. In the name of God the Father, Jesus the Son, and the Holy Spirit, he asked for guidance for steps throughout the day. He also appealed to the Holy Mother to keep them vigilant and true. After that, he gave orders to different men about the things he wanted done while he was tending to the old man and the girl at the Huntsman's Lodge.

When the meeting was dismissed, Andrew found Eve putting food and a flask in her satchel.

"I didn't expect Robin and his merry men to be Catholic," Andrew said.

"I thought you knew your history. It's in all the legends," she said. She handed him a knife in a leather sheath. "Tuck this in your belt."

"Will I need it?" he asked, worried.

"Everyone who walks in the forest should have one," she said. "You never know who or what you will meet along the way."

She stood up and Andrew saw that she had a knife too.

"Have you ever had to use yours?" he asked.

"Not on anything human," she replied and walked away.

He wondered what she meant as he fixed the knife to his belt. "Is the lodge far?" he asked, following her.

"A few miles," she said. "Why? Are you sore from yesterday?"

"A little."

She slung the satchel over her shoulder. "So was I, the first time."

The two of them trailed behind Robin and an older man named Warren the Bowman. Warren was short, with wild gray hair and a bushy beard. At first, Andrew wondered how such an old man would keep up, then realized he would have a hard time keeping up with the old man.

"Robin will ask you how you came to the forest," Eve whispered to him.

Andrew gulped hard. He hadn't thought about anyone asking him questions. "What am I supposed to tell him?"

"The truth," she said. "You have no family here, which you don't. You are an orphan like I am, which you are. We met and I brought you with me to Robin, which I did."

That is *the truth*, Andrew thought. And that's what he told Robin when the outlaw asked him a few miles later.

"I am vexed about *Hope Springs*," Robin admitted. "I have traveled the length and breadth of England and do not recall such a place. What is the nearest town or city?"

Andrew wasn't sure how to answer.

"Denver," said Eve.

Andrew gaped at Eve.

Robin's eyebrows lifted. "Denver? In Norfolk? Then, surely, I should know it."

"It is easy to miss," Eve said. "A blink and you have passed it."

Robin gave them both a skeptical look, which ended the conversation.

Andrew didn't know how many miles they walked. He was surprised that his muscles, which felt stiff at first, limbered up along the way.

From time to time, Robin made sounds like a bird call or a whistle. The same sound came back to him, as if the birds themselves were responding.

"We have men hiding all over the forest," Eve explained. "They watch for those with bad intentions, or those we know who have taken advantage of the poor."

"What do you do with them?"

"If they're really bad, we tie them up and drop them off at the nearest jail. If they are corrupt noblemen or clergy, we make them pay a toll from whatever they have."

"And then what?"

"Robin shares whatever we get with anyone in need," Eve said. "The scouts are also supposed to watch out for anyone who is lost or suffering. That's why Robin was so unhappy with Dodd."

Robin, who was several yards ahead, suddenly turned. "Wait there while Warren and I go ahead."

"Aye, Master Robin," Eve said.

"Signal if you encounter trouble," Robin said.

Eve put her fingers to her lips and gave a long shrill whistle.

"The very one," Robin said, smiling at her. He and Warren strode away.

Eve found a sturdy log just off the path and sat down. Andrew sat next to her and dug a stone out of his boot. "What's up ahead? Why did he want us to wait here?"

"He is probably going to meet up with Ket the Troll." Eve took a small waterskin from her belt and drank.

"Troll?" Andrew asked, staring at her. He imagined a very short creature that lived in rocks and mounds, like Tolkien's hobbits. "Is that just a name or is he a real troll?"

"He is a real troll." She offered the waterskin to him.

Andrew took it, but eyed her doubtfully. "You've seen him?"

She nodded. "He is very private and likes to meet with Master Robin alone."

"I thought trolls didn't like humans," Andrew said.

"They are usually shy of humans," she said. "But Robin saved the lives of Ket and his brother Hob o' the Hill. They are firm friends."

"Trolls," Andrew said thoughtfully as he took a gulp of water.

Eve knew what he was thinking. "There are a lot of things in this forest you have never seen—the kinds of things we heard about in fairy tales. They still exist in this time."

"Trolls? Giants? Pixies?"

Eve smiled at him but didn't answer.

He handed the waterskin back as a loud bird call came from somewhere ahead on the path. Eve lifted her head. "That is Robin. Come on."

She dashed off and Andrew scrambled to follow her.

Robin Hood stood in the middle of the path with a boy at his side. "It is safe to go on to the lodge," he said.

As Andrew drew closer, he realized the person next to Robin wasn't a boy, but a small man, a little shorter than Andrew, with a broad chest, and long, hairy arms and legs covered with muscle like rock. The hair on his exposed head was black, thick, and curly. He wore a cropped leather jacket, which laced in the front, and breeches that reached to his knees. He had no shoes on his big feet. His face was weather-worn and friendly.

"It is the troll," Eve whispered to Andrew.

"Meet Ket," Robin said.

"Welcome to the forest," Ket said in a low and gloomy voice. He gave Andrew a stiff bow.

"My pleasure," said Andrew, bowing in return. *He really does look like a hobbit,* he thought.

Ket gave a nod to Robin and dashed into the woods, disappearing quickly among the bushes and trees.

Andrew gave Eve a wide-eyed look. She grinned at him.

"This way," Robin said.

It was another mile before Andrew saw the lodge tucked back into a grove away from the path. The lodge was actually a shack that looked as if it had been built from whatever could be found in the woods: logs, branches, stone, mud, and leaves. Dodd was standing with Warren the Bowman, guarding the door. Dodd gave Robin an apologetic look and pushed the door open for them.

Inside, Will Scarlet sat on a stool, sharpening a knife with a stone. He stood up for Robin, who waved for him to sit again.

Reuben of Stamford lay in a crudely made bed. His daughter Ruth sat in a chair next to him. Andrew thought they already looked better and healthier than they had in the cave.

At the sight of Robin, Reuben tried to sit up.

"Save your strength," Robin said. He reached out to shake Reuben's hand, but the old man grabbed Robin's hand and kissed it instead.

"God bless you for your mercy to us," said Reuben.

Robin gently pulled his hand away. "Tell me, good man, if you have the strength: how have you fallen into such a wretched state?"

"You have heard, I am certain, of Sir Guy of Gisborne," Reuben said.

Robin snorted. "An evil-hearted fiend if ever there was one," he said.

"Then perhaps you have also heard of Alberic de Wisgar," said Reuben.

"A knight of York," Robin said. "I know of him for his hard-hearted indifference to his fellow man."

"Over time, he has borrowed a great sum of money from me," Reuben said. "As the time for repayment came, he devised a plan to destroy my ledgers and any evidence of the loans."

Robin folded his arms. "I see it all too clearly. He reasoned, in his vile mind, that destroying the ledgers would relieve him of honoring the debt. What, pray tell, did he do?"

The old man glanced at his daughter. "I wish that my dearest Ruth did not have to relive the terror of those days."

"I am not afraid, Father," Ruth said bravely.

Reuben patted his daughter's hand and said to Robin, "Alberic de Wisgar sent a mob against those of my race living in York. My daughter and I escaped, but they ransacked my home and mercilessly attacked my neighbors, wounding and killing anyone who might hand us over."

"Were they able to find your ledgers?"

"No," Reuben said. "Had Sir Alberic been thinking at all, he would have known I did not keep any records or ledgers in my home. They were kept securely with Father Barnabas, a good priest at the cathedral. It was to him that we ran for sanctuary, never believing the mob would follow us or dare to attack such a sacred place."

"Men such as Alberic de Wisgar have no regard for the sacred or the beautiful," Robin said. "What, pray tell, befell you at the cathedral?"

"One of my neighbors, beaten almost to death, revealed the hiding place of my ledgers and, thereby, gave us away. The mob stormed the cathedral, but the valiant Father Barnabas rebuked them, invoking the authority of the Church. He went so far as to threaten them with excommunication if they did not hasten to depart. The frightened mob were cowed, and they retreated. But Father Barnabas feared Sir Alberic would later enter the cathedral by stealth to murder us and steal the ledgers. The good priest believed all would be safer away from York. We sneaked away that night."

"How were you able to escape?" Will Scarlet asked.

Reuben's eyes glistened with new tears. "Thanks be to God, a man-at-arms found soldiers' cloaks to disguise us. That very night he led us out of the town by a privy gate, placing us on the road to Nottingham."

"Why then are you here rather than Nottingham?" Robin asked.

"Sir Alberic, upon discovering our escape, was enraged. He summoned the aid of Sir Guy of Gisborne and the wicked brood at Wrangby Castle to search for us. Fearing anew for our lives, we left the highway and made our way into the deepest part of the forest. Our hope was to find you before the evil assassins found us. I do not know how many days we have wandered. I know only that what little food we carried from York was gone. I fell gravely ill with a fever. Ruth discovered the cave and there we hid until your good man found us."

Robin gave an appreciative look to Will, then Eve and Andrew. "Who or what awaits you in Nottingham?" he asked. "The sheriff there is as corrupt as Sir Guy of Gisborne and Alberic de Wisgar."

Reuben clasped his hands together and pressed them to his heart. "My oldest son lives in Nottingham. Even now I fear he grieves for us as dead."

Robin put a hand on the old man's shoulder. "Take heart. One of my men shall go to his house and make it known you are safe with us. When you are strong enough, you will be united with him."

"Bless you, master, bless you!" Reuben cried out.

Will Scarlet stood and sheathed his knife. "Gladly will I go, Master Robin," he said. He looked at the old man. "You need only give me your message and tell me where I may find your kinsfolk. I shall set out posthaste."

"You will not go alone," Robin said to Will. His eyes fell on Andrew and Eve. "A meal first, before the journey."

Andrew didn't realize how hungry he had become until they sat together at a small table and devoured portions of bread, cheese, and cured meat.

Suddenly they heard shouts outside. Robin and Will were on their feet in an instant, hands on the knives in their belts.

"They have found us!" Reuben said with a pitiful cry and pulled his daughter close.

The door burst open and Little John raced in, with Warren the Bowman on his heels. "Master Robin! We found your cousin's husband, Bennett of Havelond, on the road from Scotland. He was beaten to the brink of death."

"God have mercy!" the outlaw exclaimed.

"We have taken him to the inn at Ravenswood," Little John said. "I left him in the care of the good innkeeper and well-guarded by Much the Miller's Son and Reeve the Baker."

"Did Bennett say who committed the foul deed?" Robin asked.

"No, Master. He fell into a delirium and was unable to speak." Little John's face twisted with a dark anger. "'Twas no robbery nor mere beating, Robin. The wicked assailants intended to leave him for dead. We know who is behind it, and why."

"'Tis so," Robin said. "Hasten now, Little John, to the village of Angston. Seek out Dedric, a wise physician with great skill. Bear my name and he will accompany you to the Ravenswood Inn to give what help he can to Bennett."

"Aye, Robin," Little John said.

Robin turned to Warren the Bowman. "Fly to Lady Anne at the cottage on the north side of Havelond Manor. Hob o' the Hill is already there. Under cover of darkness, bring the Lady Anne safely to me."

"'T'will be done, good master," said Warren, and he departed with Little John.

Robin spun around to Will Scarlet. "Now, Will. To this other business in Nottingham. You must have a disguise. A pilgrim's robe."

"What about us?" Eve asked.

"Beggar children are abundant there. You'll need no change of clothes," he said. "Go swiftly or you will not reach the gates before they close for the night."

Will, Eve, and Andrew were given fresh provisions and set off.

If Andrew felt confident he had the energy to travel another great distance that day, he soon repented of it.

Few people standing near Nottingham's Bridlesmith Gate would have noticed the pilgrim in the long dark robe, with his feet in ragged shoes and a staff in his hand, or the two beggar children who followed him. It was less than an hour before sunset and the three of them pressed through the crowd of people trying to get into the town, or out of it, before the gate closed for the night.

More than one person noticed the beggar boy who kept gasping and pointing at the great stone castle on the rock overlooking the town. He said words they didn't understand like "wow!" and "cool!" until he was firmly *shushed* by the beggar girl with him.

"Keep your eyes down," Eve said to Andrew. "Do not draw attention to yourself."

"But it's a *real* castle!" Andrew said back to her.

"I know, I know," Eve said, exasperated.

Will Scarlet, wearing the hood of his pilgrim's robes, stopped to look for landmarks to find the house of Silas ben Reuben. "We seek the street of the Jews," he said softly to the kids.

"A street for Jews?" Andrew said. "Why do they have their own street?" he asked, and his mind went to the Nazi regime and the Jewish ghettos it had created.

"'Tis their way, I suppose. They are secretive," Will said, but his tone betrayed that he didn't really know.

Secretive or protecting themselves or ostracized? Andrew wondered. *Which is it?* He exchanged a look with Eve. She shook her head in a better-not-to-ask way.

Will rounded a corner and stopped at the end of a narrow street. He said "aha!" and slowly counted the number of doors from the corner. Though there were people walking nearby, Andrew noticed that Will didn't ask for directions.

Andrew saw that several of the house doors were open, giving him glimpses of women at work with their laundry and sewing, and children playing nearby. Other houses were shut up, with doors and shutters closed.

Will stopped at the ninth house and waved for Andrew and Eve to come close. He tapped on the wooden door. Andrew heard a heavy click and the door slid open only a few inches. A man's dark eyes peered out at them.

"What is it you want?" the man asked.

"Silas ben Reuben," replied Will. "I have a message for him."

"How am I to know you are not a traitor who would do to me and mine as has been done to others of my people?" the man asked.

"Trust me by these words," Will said and leaned in close to the door to whisper the words he had been given by Reuben. Andrew assumed, from his classes at St. Clare's, that they were Hebrew.

Instantly bolts were slid aside and the door swung wide open. "I am Silas. Come in, friend," said a short, sturdily built man. He looked surprised to see the two children, but gestured for them to enter, then quickly checked the street before barring the door again.

He led the three of them into a small, sparsely furnished room.

"What is your message?" he asked.

Will pushed the hood of his robe back and said, "Your father, Reuben of Stamford, and your sister Ruth are safe and well."

Silas clasped his hands, bowed his head, and murmured a prayer in the same language as Will's message. "Now, thanks be to God!" he exclaimed. "Tell me of my father and sister, and how soon may I see them?"

Will told Silas the story of Reuben and Ruth. When he had finished, Silas thanked him for his kindness to his father and sister and, with a gesture for them to wait, disappeared into a back room. He returned a moment later carrying a belt of green leather, with a pattern of pearls and other precious stones.

"Your kindness is beyond recompense," Silas said. "I would have you accept this from me as a proof of my thanks to you."

"I am grateful," said Will, "but 'tis too rich a gift for me. It suits my master more."

Silas said, "Please, present it to him on my behalf. But, please, you must tell me what I may give you for your kind service." Then his eyes suddenly lit up and he said happily, "Wait!"

He dashed out of the room again and returned, unfolding a cloth. "This is a Spanish knife. They are known throughout Christendom to be of the best craftsmanship."

Will held up the knife. The blade shone a bright silver, was about six or eight inches long, and ended in a razor-sharp point. The wooden handle was ornately carved. Will examined the knife and said, with a tone of awe, "'Tis indeed of the finest make."

"Now," Silas said with hushed urgency, "we must make arrangements as to how and when I may send horses and men to meet my father and sister." He bade them to sit at a small table. "I am sorry I cannot offer you a meal, but I have sent my wife and children away to safety until I know the attack against my father will not be repeated here."

Andrew found himself sitting, then standing to stretch his stiff legs, and then pacing to keep from falling asleep.

Night had fallen by the time all things were settled.

"You must stay here until the morning," Silas said.

"Thank you," said Will, "but it would be better for us to find an inn near the gate, so we may slip away quickly when it is opened at dawn."

Silas reluctantly agreed and, with another blessing, sent the three of them on their way.

As they carefully navigated the narrow streets toward the gate, they passed a man walking the other way. Andrew noticed that the man gave Will a second glance.

Andrew looked up and saw that Will had forgotten to put the hood over his head.

They turned to one street, then another. Andrew glanced back. The man strode several yards behind them.

"He is following us," Eve whispered.

Will nodded and picked up his pace, his hand falling onto the handle of the knife under his robe.

Suddenly, another man with a long beard staggered out of an alley and tumbled into them. He grabbed onto Will's robe, as if for support, but whispered, "Friend of Silas ben Reuben, make haste. Come with me."

Will pushed the man away and said loudly, "Leave us, drunken fool!"

The man fell back into the alley, clutching at Will's robe to drag him down with him. To an outsider, it looked as if they were fighting. Andrew and Eve blocked the entrance to the alley, as if watching.

The man who'd had been following them stopped behind Eve, craning to look. Eve turned on him and held out her hand. "Can you spare a few florins, sir?"

The man pushed her aside.

"Ale!" the bearded man cried out. He still had hold of Will's robes, pleading with him.

"You have had enough for one night," Will said to him. "Let go of me."

Eve said loudly to Andrew, "Summon a guard."

Andrew wasn't sure if she was serious or not.

With the word "guard," the man in the street looked alarmed and moved quickly away.

When he was out of sight, Eve said, "He is gone."

The bearded man let go of Will, who helped him to his feet. They clasped hands in friendship. "Come this way."

He led them down the alley to another passage. At the end of that was a door, which he opened noiselessly. Will, Andrew, and Eve followed him into a dark and low-ceilinged hall. They then came to an open courtyard. Andrew felt a night breeze blowing upon his face. He looked up and saw stars twinkling as brightly as he'd ever seen in his life.

"Go through the door on the left," said the bearded man. "'T'will lead you to the Fletcher Gate."

"I thank you, friend," said Will.

The bearded man retreated into a different passage.

They went through the doorway on the left and, in only a few steps, came to a street. They followed it to the Fletcher Gate. Nearby, an inn leaned precariously toward the city wall, as if it were trying to peek over the top.

The landlord asked Will no questions, nor did he speak to the two children. Will's money seemed to be the only thing he cared about.

There was a common room with a few rough-hewn tables. Three men sat at one near a small window and talked loudly, laughing and hitting their fists against the table top.

Will went to a table in a back corner and took the seat facing the room and the entrance. The kids sat with their backs to the door. A moment later the innkeeper approached and took orders for their supper and drinks. The supper turned out to be a stew that Andrew couldn't identify.

Two more men arrived and sat at a nearby table. Andrew saw them out of the corner of his eye. They were big fellows, dressed in well-made tunics and leggings. He assumed they were the servants of a nobleman. They bent across the table to speak in low voices, which made Andrew want to listen even more closely.

With his eyes on Will, who looked wearily at the three men by the window, Andrew heard the names "Alberic" and "Reuben." He noticed that Will tipped his head ever so slightly, glancing at Andrew to indicate he'd also heard them.

Andrew turned toward the two men, bending as if to adjust his boot. One man had dark shaggy hair hanging over a craggy face. The second man was bald, with a broad face and an angry scar circling his right eye.

The door to the inn opened and a man strode in with a loud stomping of his boots on the wooden floor. Andrew sat up again, turning quickly to glance at the newcomer. It was the young man with the beard Andrew had seen at Havelond.

Eve nudged Andrew. "Maurice, the son of Sir Reynauld," she whispered.

Andrew gave a sharp nod.

"There you are," Maurice said and marched over to the two men.

"Greetings, my lord," the craggy-faced man said.

Maurice sat down at the table. "Fools!" he said. "One small task and you failed!"

"My lord!" protested the scar-faced man.

Maurice's voice dropped low. Andrew strained to listen and heard him say in a sneering tone, "Bennett of Havelond is alive."

"Impossible," the craggy-faced man said. "No man could have survived that beating."

Maurice growled. "Even now he is being cared for at the Ravenswood Inn. You must go without delay and finish the job for which you were hired."

The scar-face man stammered, "My lord, with respect, we have been given new orders from Sir Alberic."

"What is that to me?" asked Maurice.

"We are his servants and duty-bound to him," the craggy-faced man said. "You will remember, I am sure, that he lent us to your father's service out of respect."

"What will Sir Alberic say when he learns you did not perform that service?" asked Maurice.

Andrew could hear the men shuffle nervously.

"I shall see to Bennett at Ravenswood," the craggy-faced man offered, then said to the scar-faced man, "You remain here in Nottingham to keep watch over the house of Silas. Reuben will undoubtedly send a message to his son."

The scar-faced man nodded.

"What is this? Tell me of what you speak," Maurice insisted.

The two men took turns explaining about Sir Alberic's hunt for Reuben and the discovery of an eldest son in Nottingham.

"Why seek the son?" asked Maurice. "Where is the old Jew?"

The craggy-faced man said, "The outlaw Robin Hood harbors Reuben somewhere in the forest. There is no finding him without battling the outlaw and his men."

Maurice was silent for a moment, then said, "I shall go with you to Ravenswood, to ensure that you do not fail again. Bennett of Havelond must not leave that inn alive."

"We shall go nowhere tonight," the scar-faced man said. "The gates are closed."

"As we are here, let us eat and drink and be friends," the craggy-faced man said.

"We shall eat and drink together," said Maurice sourly. "But we are not friends."

Andrew saw out of the corner of his eye that Maurice now turned in his chair to observe the room. His gaze fell on Will Scarlet for a moment, then he turned back to his own table. The innkeeper came to take their order.

Will signaled the kids and they rose. Down a short hall, they climbed a flight of rickety stairs to an upper floor with several rooms. The three of them went into the one closest to the stairs. A single lamp on a small table offered more shadow than light to the dingy chamber. There were no beds, only mats of straw scattered on the floor.

"We are supposed to sleep in here?" Andrew asked, aware of a foul odor coming from somewhere, or everywhere.

Will pointed to two piles of straw nearest a long wall. "The finest accommodations," he said to them. "I shall return in due time." He slipped out of the door again.

Andrew sat down on the bed of straw. It pricked him in the backside. He tried to adjust the lumps. Nothing helped. So, he pushed at the mat to serve as a makeshift pillow and stretched out on the floor. *A hot shower*, he thought wistfully. *Modern mattresses, air conditioning, pillows, clean floors, lighting...* His gaze went to a small round pot in the corner. He shuddered to think what it was used for. He groaned.

"You will get used to it," Eve whispered. She sat on her mat and placed her satchel at the top end as a pillow.

Andrew kicked off one boot, then the other, and rubbed his feet, aware of the callouses forming on the heels and balls of his feet. He lay back. Black wooden beams crisscrossed the ceiling. He remembered seeing similar beams in a restaurant in Denver. The owner said the beams were once part of an ancient pub in England. Andrew wondered if the ancient pub had been located in Nottingham. *How strange would it be if I am now looking at the same beams that wound up in Denver hundreds of years later?*

"How does time work?" he asked Eve.

She groaned. "You want to talk about that *now*?"

"Why not?" Andrew said. The dim flicker of the lamplight made the grooves in the wood shift and change. "What did Alfred Virtue say about time? He must have come up with a few ideas, since he was jumping all over it."

Eve sighed, then said, "Alfred Virtue wrote in his journal that time may be like the surface of a lake."

Andrew thought of the pond he had sat next to that morning.

"He said that time is there, smooth and peaceful," Eve continued. "But then something drops into the water and the surface ripples out in little waves."

"Ripples and waves," Andrew repeated.

She said, "Small grains of sand will make tiny ripples that spread out a little bit. And big rocks make bigger ripples that spread further out. The grains of sand or the bigger rocks are like the different kinds of events that happen in time."

Andrew cradled his arms behind his head. "So, an event like World War II would be like dropping a giant rock in the water," he said.

"That's right. It makes *huge* ripples that affect everything around it," Eve said.

"What about a normal life?" Andrew asked. "Is that a tiny grain of sand?"

"What is normal?" she asked. "If you grow up to be an Albert Einstein or a Saint Francis or a guy who sets off a nuclear explosion, then you have made a big ripple. But I guess that most of our lives are like tiny grains of sand, affecting only what is close by."

Andrew studied the ridges in the cracks of the wooden ceiling. "The top of a lake is almost never smooth," he said.

"What?"

"The water is almost never smooth," Andrew repeated. He turned and propped himself up on his elbow to face her. "Time is always rippling because stuff is always being dropped into it, like rain."

Eve was sitting against the wall. She folded her arms and frowned at him. "The idea is still the same, though. Small ripples, big ripples, a lot of ripples. Go to sleep." She lay down on the mat.

Andrew rolled onto his back again and tried to find a comfortable position. He couldn't.

The door opened again, and Will Scarlet walked softly in. He gestured for both Andrew and Eve not to speak and extinguished the lamp. Pale moonlight came through a single small window on the far wall. Andrew saw the shadow of Will Scarlet slide down to the floor beneath the window.

Andrew squinted against the darkness.

Will whispered, "The men below are the very scoundrels Robin wants to meet. Alas, we are unable to send word to him, or capture them. We must bide our time until the morrow." He folded his arms across his chest.

Andrew squirmed and thought the bed of leaves and a pillow made of a tree root was more comfortable than this.

A harsh whisper of "Andrew!" in his ear brought him awake. Suddenly hands were on his arm, shaking him until he turned over.

He opened his eyes to see Eve crouching over him. "What's wrong?" he asked.

Another voice—a man's—demanded, "Who are you?"

Startled, Andrew sat up. The man who had followed them the night before was standing in front of Will Scarlet.

Will was on his knees, cowering. "I am but a poor pilgrim who journeys to the holy shrine at Walsingham." He sounded afraid, but Andrew noticed that his hand was on his hip, the hilt of the Spanish knife within easy reach.

A gray light came through the small window on the wall.

"A pilgrim?" shouted the man from the street. He laughed derisively. "A pilgrim's robe covering a rogue's body."

"I was not always a pilgrim," Will said. "Our Lord works in the stoniest of hearts."

"And to whom do these children belong?" the man asked.

"They are beggars. I have allowed them to travel with me, out of Christian charity."

Andrew noticed Mr. Craggy Face and Mr. Scar Face, the two servants of Sir Alberic, standing in the doorway. They peered in with sleepy eyes.

The man snorted. "Why were you on the street of the Jews?"

To this, the men at the door straightened up. "Say that again?" the craggy-faced one said.

"This is none of your affair," the man from the street said to him.

"How, sir, is it your affair?" Will asked the man from the street.

"'Tis my affair because I am Cobb the Brewer and I know you are not a pilgrim, but one of the band of cutthroats that serves the outlaw Robin Hood! You were at his side in the forest, where I was stopped and relieved of half of my purse."

"You are mistaken, sir," Will said. "Though, if the outlaw took any of your purse, it was because you gave him cause."

Cobb sneered at him. "As I would expect one of his rogues to say! Come downstairs. The captain of the guard will determine whether I am mistaken or not."

Will tipped his head to Andrew and Eve to come along and crossed the room.

The two men at the door stepped aside as the three followed Cobb into the hall and down the stairs. Andrew noticed that Eve grabbed her satchel, returning it to her shoulder.

The servants of Sir Alberic stayed closely on their heels. All of them entered the common room, where two men sat at a table.

"Captain!" Cobb the Brewer called out.

The two men rose from the table. Long swords hung at both their sides. One man was thin with a twisted nose and small bird-like eyes. He wore a blue and gold robe that made him look like an official. Andrew assumed he was the captain. The second man wore a silver hauberk and drew his sword.

"Who have you there?" the captain asked.

Cobb said, "He declares himself a pilgrim, Captain, but I know him to be an outlaw in league with Robin Hood."

"Show me your hands," the captain said to Will. "Then I will know if you are a pilgrim or something else."

Will hesitated.

The captain stepped forward and grabbed Will's hands. He yanked them into view, inspecting the left and then the right. "Callouses and corns. You are no stranger to archery."

At that moment the door burst open and the innkeeper, with a bucket in hand, bustled in.

The open door was enough for Will to shout to Andrew and Eve, "Run!"

Andrew sprang forward but bumped into the captain and fell. Eve darted straight through the men to the door, pausing for a second to turn to check on Andrew. Andrew half-crawled toward her.

The innkeeper, startled by the commotion, dropped the bucket and fell back against the door, closing it again. Andrew reached Eve, but they were stuck as the innkeeper stumbled one way, then another. Andrew glanced back and saw that Will was now in the clutches of Sir Alberic's servants. They pulled at his arms, but he slammed a heel onto the foot of one and gave a sharp elbow to the other. They reeled back and he threw himself at the door.

The innkeeper shrieked and tried to step out of the way.

The five men came after Will, but he seized the dropped bucket by the handle and swung it around, striking Cobb on the side of the head. Knocked senseless, Cobb fell back into the captain and the guard, then onto the floor, effectively blocking the way for Sir Alberic's servants.

Eve and Andrew struggled with the rusty latch on the door as Will swung the bucket again, driving the five men back.

Andrew managed to lift the latch and began to pull the door open just as the captain pushed the craggy-faced servant hard at Will. Both men slammed against the door, closing it again. Now Will, Andrew, Eve, the craggy-faced man, and the innkeeper were heaped up there. Andrew dropped to the floor and crawled to one side. Eve did the same, crawling to the other.

Will struggled against the weight of the craggy-faced man, who was trying to regain his balance. The innkeeper, who was stronger than he looked, let out a grunt and pushed both Will and Mr. Craggy Face back toward the room. The captain and the guard caught hold of Will's robe and, tripping over the still-fallen Cobb, crashed to the floor. Andrew saw the Spanish knife fly from Will's belt. It hit the floor and slid under a table. Andrew scurried after it, unseen by anyone in the fight.

The captain and the guard pinned Will's shoulders to the floor. The scar-faced servant pounced, landing on Will's kicking legs.

"Ropes! Bring me ropes!" the captain shouted at the innkeeper.

The innkeeper looked startled. "Rope? Do I have rope? Where do I keep it?" he muttered and ran back and forth.

"The sheriff will hear of your thick wits!" the captain yelled at the innkeeper. The craggy-faced man was now on his feet, ready to attack if Will tried anything.

"Have mercy, good captain!" cried the innkeeper as he fumbled loudly behind a counter.

Cobb dragged himself to a wall and propped himself up, rubbing the side of his head.

The innkeeper banged around, finding nothing helpful. Finally, Mr. Craggy Face pushed him aside and went to a back room. He returned seconds later with a coil of rope and scowled at the innkeeper as he threw it to the captain.

Andrew crouched near a table and looked at Eve for help. Should they attack the men to help Will? Should they run?

Eve, standing near the closed door, lifted her hand ever so slightly as a signal for Andrew to wait.

Will's arms were roughly bound, the knots pulled tight. The captain and the guard yanked him to his feet.

Just then Maurice, son of Sir Reynauld, came down the stairs, adjusting his tunic as if he'd just awakened. "This is a riotous place," he complained.

"Open the door," the captain commanded the innkeeper.

The innkeeper obliged, jerking the door open wide. A small crowd had gathered outside but quickly scattered as the captain and guard pushed Will Scarlet out. Cobb, still rubbing his head, followed.

The two servants raced over to Maurice and whispered, with grand gestures, what had just happened.

Maurice's eyes lit up. "That outlaw may solve both of our problems," Maurice said. "Get out of my way." He pushed past them and marched through the doorway.

Eve signaled for Andrew to follow, but the innkeeper stepped in front of them and closed the door. "Wait," he said. "I am a friend to Robin and the Men of the Greenwood."

Andrew and Eve looked at one another, surprised.

The innkeeper dropped into a chair and fanned his face with his apron. "Be a good lass and bring me a cup of ale."

Eve went behind the counter and soon had the drink in the innkeeper's hand. He gulped it down. "If you know how to find the outlaw, then be quick. Tell him about his friend," he said.

"What will they do to Will?" Andrew asked.

"He will be hanged if no one comes to his aid."

Eve turned to Andrew, "You stay here. I will go to Robin."

Andrew felt the blood drain from his face. "Stay here? Alone?"

"I am the faster runner and know the way," Eve said. "You need to keep an eye on Will—and Maurice."

"But . . ." Andrew glanced at the innkeeper, whose head was tilted back and his eyes closed. "The *stone*. If you go and something happens, how will I get home?"

She brought out the chain from her neck. "You hold onto it."

This idea scared him even more. "What if I lose it?"

"You cannot have it both ways," Eve said. "Take it or leave it."

"You keep it," Andrew said, swallowing hard. "Go. I will stay here. Alone."

With his eyes still closed, the innkeeper said, "You won't be alone, lad."

It wasn't hard for Andrew to catch up to Will Scarlet. The parade of the captain, Cobb, Maurice, and the two servants drew a lot of attention as they made their way through the streets. Guards had now joined their captain in the march. Andrew overheard the captain asking the names of their party, to serve as witnesses. The craggy-faced servant was Jenkins of Dove's Field. The bald, scar-faced man was Walter of Larimore. Maurice gave his own name with a tone of great significance, but the captain didn't seem to notice.

The captain stopped to turn and announce, "I am Captain Butcher, second in command to the Lord Sheriff of Nottingham. As the Lord Sheriff is in London for a fortnight, I am in command and will administer justice."

Will snorted at the word "justice."

It was a short walk to the gray stone building that served as the town's prison. Will was dragged inside by the captain and the guard, with Cobb following. The captain told the rest to wait. He pushed the door closed, but Maurice held it fast with his hand.

"I have an interest in your prisoner," Maurice said.

Captain Butcher looked him over as if seeing him for the first time. "I shall be the judge of that." A handful of guards assembled in front of the doorway, pushing back Maurice and the crowd.

"Keep order here," the captain said and slammed the door in their faces. The crowd milled for a few moments until, seeing there would be no further drama, they slowly went their separate ways.

Andrew moved off to the side, as close to the door as he could get. He crouched down next to the wall, mud and filth threatening to cover his boot tops. He thought he smelled rotten vegetables.

There were occasional shouts from inside. Maurice, Jenkins, and Walter moved a few yards down the street and conferred among themselves.

A half hour went by, then an hour. The door eventually opened again and the captain stepped out. The guards—five of them—snapped to attention. "The prisoner is defiant," he said to anyone who was listening. "He has told us to do our worst to him, and so we shall."

"What are your orders?" one of the guards asked.

Captain Butcher gave a sinister smile. "Prepare the gallows for him! He shall swing at dawn."

The guards saluted and marched away.

Andrew sprang to his feet. "You are going to hang him? Without a trial?"

The captain glanced at him like a man surprised that a monkey could speak.

"Go before I have you arrested as well," he said.

Andrew took a few steps, as if to obey, but looked past the captain. He saw Will inside, being punched and dragged to an inner door. Will kept a proud look as they manhandled him into a passage, and then he was gone.

The captain glared at Andrew. Andrew backed away into the shadow of an empty animal pen that had partially collapsed against a wall. He tried to disappear behind the last standing post.

"Captain Butcher!" Maurice shouted, striding forward. "By what authority do you hang this man? It is for the sheriff alone to render such a judgment."

"I am the sheriff when the sheriff is away," Captain Butcher said simply.

"I beseech you to allow me inside so I might have a word with you," Maurice said.

"If you must speak, then do so here," the captain said brusquely.

Maurice glanced around. He gave a stern look at Andrew, who ducked behind the post. "I have a way for you to capture Robin Hood himself," he said.

The captain's eyebrows shot up. "Speak," he said. "'Tis a fair reward to have that rogue imprisoned or, better still, slain."

"It is this," said Maurice, and his villainous face took on a crafty look. "Do not hang this man here, but in Ravenswood."

"Ravenswood? What does Ravenswood have to do with this business?"

"A man dear to the outlaw's heart lies there, ill to the point of death. The outlaw will surely go there to aid him. Yet, it is a surer thing if his fellow outlaw is taken there to be hanged. The outlaw will come and, when he does, you and your men will capture him. Think of it, captain. *Two* hangings rather than one."

The captain was thoughtful for a moment, then asked, "Who did you say you are?"

"I am Maurice, son of Sir Reynauld of Prestbury and ally to Sir Alberic de Wisgar. You know them as men of nobility, men who show lavish gratitude to those who assist their cause."

The captain straightened up. "Is that so?"

"The man who lies ill is a hindrance to my father's interests."

"And Sir Alberic?"

"The outlaw harbors a fugitive, a Jew who runs from Sir Alberic de Wisgar's demand for justice."

"What fugitive?"

"Reuben of Stamford."

"The father of Silas?" Captain Butcher suddenly looked to the left and the right, as if he feared who might be listening. "Come inside," he said to Maurice.

The two men went inside and closed the door. Jenkins and Walter came near, pressing close to the door to hear what was being said inside. A few moments later, the door opened again and Maurice stepped onto the dirty street. He had a smug look on his face.

"My lord?" Jenkins asked.

"The man is a dolt. A sheep's head," Maurice said under his breath.

"What are we to do?" Walter asked. "My master will be angry if I do not find the home of Silas ben Reuben."

"Put Silas ben Reuben out of your mind," Maurice snapped. "The captain has agreed to take the outlaw's man to Ravenswood."

"My lord, I fear you have not considered the violent skill of the outlaw's men," said Jenkins. "They may ambush us in Ravenswood."

"The captain assures me that he will take more than enough men to do battle and capture the scoundrel," Maurice said. "They will not all march with us, but many will take to the surrounding forest. He believes his guards are as crafty as the Men of the Greenwood. If he is true to his word, all will come to a satisfactory end."

Andrew slid down behind the pole. His mind raced as he drew his knees up and embraced them with his folded arms. What was he to do? How could he get a message to Robin Hood about this scheme?

He heard the scuff of footfall on the dirt next to him. He looked up. Maurice stood in front of him.

"Spare something from your purse for a poor beggar boy?" Andrew asked, holding up his hand.

"Your clothes are not that of a beggar, nor is your manner of speech," Maurice said. "You are a spy for the outlaw."

Andrew was about to protest, but Maurice reached down and caught Andrew's collar in a firm grip. He jerked the boy up and leaned in close. "You will journey with us to Ravenswood."

Eve ran as fast as she could from Nottingham, racing north to the forest she was growing to know and love so well. She had become used to running long distances but now felt as if her legs were turning to rubber and a rib had turned inward to stab at her side. More than any fatigue from running, she felt the weight of leaving Andrew behind. Guilt pressed on her for tricking him into traveling back in time.

It wasn't clear to her—even Alfred Virtue wasn't entirely sure—what happened if a time traveler was hurt.

A mile into the woods, she heard a birdcall, a familiar signal. She whistled the call of a whip-poor-will in response, a tricky effort.

Nidd of Whitby leapt down from a nearby tree, clumsily landing on a thick root and stumbling. "Greetings to you, Waif of the Woods," he said, quickly recovering.

"Greetings, Nidd," she said, breathless. "I have urgent news for Robin from Nottingham."

"By God's grace, he is not far," Nidd said. "He is now in Hares Hollow, meeting with his cousin Anne. Come."

Nidd dashed away. Eve groaned as she clutched her side and chased after him.

Hares Hollow was the name of a thicket that, to the untrained eye, wasn't noticeable from any nearby path. Its landmark was an ancient willow that stood in the center, its thin branches lazily spread out in a broad canopy that reached to the ground. Over a dozen people could sit inside that canopy without being seen.

Eve approached and Nidd, who had arrived first, pushed an arm into the cascading leaves and spread them apart for Eve to enter.

Robin and his cousin Lady Anne sat inside on crude stumps that had been brought in to serve as chairs. Lady Anne's back was to Eve, but Robin saw her clearly and gestured for her to wait.

Lady Anne was saying, "Good cousin, why have you brought me here when my husband is in Ravenswood?" She sounded anxious.

Robin said in a soothing tone, "To be assured you were not followed by any of Sir Reynauld's allies. To lead them to your husband through you, my lady, would endanger both your lives."

"Murder?" Anne shook her head. "Evil as he may be, I cannot believe Sir Reynauld is capable of that."

"My dearest lady," Robin said, "Sir Reynauld had your husband savagely beaten and left for dead. You must not be naïve about his capabilities."

"Why?" she cried out. "For Havelond? Is a house and land worth condemning his immortal soul?"

"I fear he is not a man who cares about his soul," Robin said sadly. "Havelond is superior in every way to his own house and lands in Prestbury. He is determined to keep his hold on it."

"What can I do?" she asked, her voice choking with tears.

"Dearest cousin, you must trust me. I will give Sir Reynauld good cause to return to Prestbury. He will also pay the price for inflicting such pain on you and your husband."

"When may I see my husband?" she asked.

"We shall go under the cloak of darkness. Rest now, refresh yourself," Robin said. He turned his attention to Eve. "Come forward, Waif of the Woods. Tell me all. Where is Will Scarlet and your friend?"

Eve knelt at his feet. "Sad news, Master Robin," she said, and told him everything about meeting Reuben's son and Will being taken to the prison.

Robin leapt up. "This is grave news indeed."

"There is more," Eve said, and added what she knew about Maurice and the two servants from Sir Alberic. "Master Robin, Maurice knows Bennett is recovering at Ravenswood."

Robin looked at her, wide-eyed, then shot like an arrow through the curtain of branches. Eve and Anne looked at one another, surprised. Eve helped Anne to her feet, and they followed him.

In the open again, Eve heard Robin summoning the men to his side.

"What, pray tell, does this mean?" Lady Anne asked her cousin. "What has Sir Reynauld to do with Sir Alberic? I do not know the man."

Eve gave a sympathetic look to Anne. "Sir Alberic's servants beat your husband, my lady."

Anne gasped, clasping her hands together. "Why? Why would two of his servants carry out that evil task?"

"It was a favor," Eve said.

"Evil men readily aid one another in their foul conspiracies," Robin said. "This is a troublesome alliance. If Sir Alberic's men are in league with Sir Reynauld, then Sir Alberic must have something to gain."

Over a dozen men had now gathered. Robin raised his hand to bid them to silence and said, "Lads, good honest Will Scarlet has been seized in Nottingham. What say you?"

"He must be rescued!" came the fierce cry. "If we have to pull down every stone of Nottingham town, we will save him!" The hard looks on the faces of the outlaws showed their resolution.

"We may also suffer hardship in Ravenswood if we are not diligent," Robin said. Then he gave assignments to the various men, sending some men to Ravenswood to protect Bennett and others to devise a means to rescue Will from Nottingham. Once that was done, he proclaimed, "With our Lord's help, Will shall be rescued and brought safely back amongst us!"

"Or many a mother's son of Nottingham shall be slain," a voice in the crowd called out.

"Pray it does not come to that," Robin said.

Anne came alongside Robin and put a hand on his arm. "I implore you, cousin. Spare the innocent from a deed that was none of their doing. Allow me, for my part, to seek justice according to the law."

Robin turned to her, a skeptical look on his face. "How will you accomplish such a miracle, my lady?"

"I shall go forthwith to the Abbey of Saint Mary's and appeal to the abbot himself," she replied.

A few men laughed. Robin gave a harsh look to silence them. He said to her, "You will not receive justice from the abbot, good lady. He is corrupt to the very core of his being."

"I must try," she said.

Robin relented. "You will not reach the abbot tonight, but with good speed, you may arrive in the morning."

"And if the sheriff hangs Will Scarlet while she makes a vain appeal?" Nidd called out.

"The sheriff is not there. He has gone to London," a man named Brawby said. "Captain Butcher is in command, a man worthy of his name. He will do anything to advance his position in the eyes of his superiors. If hanging Will Scarlet will gain him status, he will do it."

"We must go! We must attack!" the men cried out.

Robin waved his hands for calm. "To attack Nottingham would be an act of war. If we are to go to war, then we must do so based on a just cause. Remember, *we* are the outlaws in this fight."

More shouts erupted from the gathering. "Are we to do nothing?" was the prevailing cry.

Robin spoke over them: "While my cousin seeks out the abbot, I will send Geoffrey the Palmer, our fastest runner, to scout out Nottingham. Only then may we discern a course of action."

Geoffrey the Palmer, a tall man with the longest legs Eve had ever seen on a human, pushed through the assembly. He said, "Master Robin, give me leave to depart now or I shall not arrive before the gates close for the night."

"Go," Robin said. "Enter by way of the Fletcher Gate. Seek out Harold, the innkeeper there. He will know what has become of Will. He also knows how to aid your escape, though the gate be closed. Report to me in Ravenswood."

"Aye, Master Robin." Geoffrey turned, making his way back through the men and onward into the woods.

"My dear lady," Robin said to Anne. "To meet the abbot, you must go to York. If you hope to be there on the morrow, you must forgo seeing your husband in Ravenswood tonight."

She looked at him gravely. "I know, cousin. If it will save further bloodshed, then I must yield my own heart's desire."

He took her hands in his. "You, good lady, are a saint."

She clasped his hands in return, her eyes filled with tears of sorrow. "I am not as yet. God willing, I will become one."

Robin said, "Summon your servant. You must depart."

"My servant fled in fear when she heard of my husband's beating," Anne said.

Robin turned to Eve. "Evangeline, you will ride with Anne as her servant."

"Me?" she asked. "But what about Andrew? He remains in Nottingham."

"You are of no help to him even if you returned to Nottingham. Geoffrey will bring us news," Robin said. "Go with Lady Anne."

"Yes, Master Robin," she said, though her heart sank at the thought of Andrew making his way in such a strange world.

Robin smiled at her, then turned and called out, "On your knees, men and women of good faith. Let us ask for our Lady's protection and help in what we must do, believing our cause to be just."

They knelt, performing the Sign of the Cross as Robin began to pray. It was a very short appeal to Mary and all the saints for their aid. Eve was a Catholic and sometimes prayed in this way, but only now did she feel it as a burning in her heart.

They finished and Robin quickly stood up. "Look lively, good friends! We do not know what time we have, nor what we face in the day to come! But by the grace of God, we shall face all things well."

Eve lost track of the time as they journeyed to York. The afternoon light drained away to the night and she found it harder and harder to stay awake. She nodded off more than once as her horse trudged along, and only occasionally did she see the shadows of small villages and a house or two in the distant darkness. Robin had sent Nidd to accompany them. Eve marveled at his attentiveness to every movement and sound around them, his hand ready on his sword, or reaching for his longbow.

They eventually came to the Barstone Inn, not far from York. Nidd knew the owners well and believed it was best for the Lady Anne to have rest, if only for a couple of hours, before meeting the abbot. Eve felt like she sleepwalked from the front door of the inn to a spacious room in the back. Lady Anne collapsed onto a framed bed. Eve fell onto a mattress stuffed with feathers on the floor.

She dreamt of her own bed at home and, in her dream, wondered why she had ever come to a place without paved roads and cars and comfortable hotels and electricity and running water.

The dream ended when Nidd shook her shoulder. "Up, good waif. Attend to your lady."

Eve stood up, swaying where she stood, feeling as if she hadn't slept at all. She drew the curtains on two large windows, allowing a dim gray light into the room.

The Lady Anne was sitting on the side of her bed.

"What may I do for you, my lady?" Eve asked, holding back a yawn.

"Fetch water for the pitcher and bowls," she said.

Eve looked around and saw that the room had not only the expected bed and stand, but also a small table and chairs, a bench near yet another window, a wardrobe, and a small room for storage at the back. Eve was about to go to the door when the door suddenly flew open.

A thin woman bustled in with a pitcher and bowl. "Good morrow," she said. "I am Margaret, wife of the proprietor. Water for your washing. I shall bring food anon."

Margaret left and, several minutes later, returned with plates of bread, cold meat, and cups of ale. She placed them on the small table and said, "Ring the bell when you have finished," and pointed to a bell hanging by the door. Eve and the Lady Anne ate in a sleepy silence.

Nidd came to the door and reported, "The gates of York are opened. We must hurry to the Abbey of Saint Mary's or the crowds will reach the abbot ahead of us."

Eve and Lady Anne hurriedly ate and were soon on the road again.

York was an ancient city, with Roman walls and gates, narrow roads, and a shamble of shacks that served as houses and shops. Eve had to dodge the occasional sheep or sidestep a tradesman pulling a cart. Nidd led the way, with a new man, Hal the Smith, following several steps behind them. Nidd explained that Hal was an old friend and often served as Robin's eyes and ears in York. Hal was short and elderly, with dozy eyes and sagging cheeks. But when he helped Eve onto her horse, she detected a great strength in his unassuming body. He did not speak the entire journey.

The Abbey of Saint Mary's sat along a river. Walls with arches and gates enclosed the grounds. Eve expected it to be a quiet place of prayer and meditation, but it was bustling with servants, tradesmen, workers, and laypeople who had come for reasons of their own.

As they crossed a vast courtyard, the Lady Anne explained that the abbey had dozens of Benedictine monks, scholars, and a school for boys. "It is a rich abbey," she said, lowering her voice. "Some say it is too rich, tempting the abbot to lavish self-indulgences."

"Aye, my lady," Nidd said. "A gathering of holy men rebelled, demanding a change to a simpler life. They were cast out and formed their own haven, the Fountains Abbey, to the north and east of here."

"Nidd?" a voice called out.

Nidd turned. A young man wearing a black robe crossed the courtyard. He smiled and stretched out his hand to shake.

"Father Simon," Nidd said and clasped the young man's hand.

The priest pulled him close, his smile held frozen while he said, "Why have you come to this lion's den?" His whisper was harsh. "What if you are recognized?"

"Who would recognize a poor peasant like myself?" Nidd asked in the same whisper. "I accompany the Lady Anne, at my master's bidding. She is his cousin and in need of help."

Father Simon stepped back. He bowed to Lady Anne. "My lady, welcome."

Lady Anne curtsied in return.

"Father Simon has been our spiritual guide in the Greenwood," Nidd explained, never raising his voice. "He hears our many confessions and offers the Mass. He is a great comfort to us."

Father Simon saw Eve and cried out, "Our dear Waif of the Woods!"

Eve smiled and curtsied.

Father Simon turned to Nidd again and asked, "Pray tell, why are you here?"

Nidd stepped closer to the priest and quickly told him why they'd come to the abbey.

Father Simon nodded. "The abbot conducts his business in the chapter house. I shall take you there," he said. "There is already a vast assembly of men and women at the door, waiting to pay their rents with money or goods. Others come to appear in answer to some charge or demand made by the abbot, or by one of the knights who manage his lands. Most come with complaints about the abbot's bailiffs or the stewards who have oppressed them."

"How is it that an abbey, dedicated as it is to the love of Christ, would employ oppressive bailiffs?" Lady Anne asked.

Father Simon lowered his head. "'Tis a question often asked, but never answered."

They passed from the courtyard through a doorway and into a broad hall. It was just as Father Simon had said: a crowd of men and women, mostly in peasants' clothing, were there.

"Follow me," Father Simon said and pushed through the crowd.

Some of the people assumed he was a man of importance and began to ask him for help. Others thrust parchments at him, asking if he'd give them to the abbot. He held up his hands, apologizing again and again as they pressed on. "Allow the *lady* through, if you please!" he said.

"Are we cheating by going to the front?" Eve asked Nidd.

Nidd looked puzzled by her question. "Knights and ladies are always to be heard first."

Soon they reached a set of double doors. Two taller guards stood straight with even taller spears held upright.

They suddenly crossed the spears to block the door. "No further," one said.

"The Lady Anne of Havelond is here to see the abbot," Father Simon said.

The guards lifted the spears and stepped aside. "Tell the prior," the one said.

Father Simon slipped in, closing the door behind him. A moment later he returned and gave an encouraging nod. "We are to wait here."

They moved to the side.

Eve was crowded close to Father Simon. She looked at the young, clean-shaven face, the kind eyes that scanned the crowd in the hall, and the thin lips that moved ever so slightly. His hands were clasped in front of his chest.

Father Simon met her gaze. He smiled.

Eve asked, "Are you praying?"

"They are in most need of it," he replied.

An hour went by as the door opened and a short bald man wearing a white robe summoned various people to enter. Most entered with expressions of hope but came out with looks of sadness or anger.

Finally, the bald man called out for "Lady Anne of Havelond."

"This is where I bid you *adieu*," Father Simon said. "My presence will only hurt your case. The abbot and I often disagree."

Lady Anne thanked him, and the priest began his journey through the crowd again, waving away more parchments and appeals.

"I shall await you in the courtyard," Nidd said.

Lady Anne, with Eve close behind, was led into the large meeting room. The Abbot Robert sat behind a table covered with parchments. He was a plump man with curved lips that moved readily from a pout to a sneer. His red face was like a cascade, his forehead rolling down to pig-like eyes, thick jowls rolling to a double chin that then rolled over the collar of his robe. He looked fierce and unhappy. Next to him was the prior, his second in command, whose slender face and sad eyes contrasted sharply with the abbot's appearance.

To the right of the abbot sat the sheriff of York, along with two severe-looking knights.

"A pack of grumbling rascals," the abbot complained loudly and threw a parchment aside. "What am I to do with them?"

"My lord abbot," the prior responded in a calm and steady voice, "when wrongs are charged against the stewards of the abbey, we must reflect up on the honor and grace of the Holy Virgin, after whom our house is named. If our servants are shown to have acted without mercy, they should be punished."

"Save your breath, prior, for I would rather leave my bailiffs to do as they think needful than meddle in matters of which I know little." The abbot turned a squinty eye to the prior. "If things were left to you, we should all go naked and give these rascals all that they craved. Say no more. I am abbot and, while I am chief of this house, I will do as it seems fit."

The abbot looked up at the Lady Anne and was about to speak when the doors crashed open and a tall man strode in. He was dressed in a hauberk, with a sword slung from his belt. On his head of rough black hair was a hat of velvet, which he lifted as he entered. Behind him came his squire, bearing his helmet and a heavy mace.

The abbot half-rose in his seat. "Sir Guy," he said with a gurgling cough of a laugh, "you have come at last."

"There are one or two cases I wish to hear," Sir Guy said with a very sudden and sharp glance at Lady Anne. He dropped into a vacant chair at the table. "One involves that villainous robber and murderer Robin Hood."

"My lord sheriff," the abbot said, turning to the sheriff of York, "we look to you to take stronger measures than you have. You must root out the band of vipers in Barnsdale."

"Barnsdale or Sherwood?" the sheriff replied with a disdainful sniff. "He seems to be in both forests at the same time."

"He must be found, wherever he has nested," Sir Guy said. "His deeds are an offense to all men of nobility."

The prior coughed gently and said, "Yet, if I am bold, Sir Guy, his deeds are no worse than deeds done by barons and lords to the poor of our county this past year.

None of them ever received punishment from you, my lord sheriff."

Sir Guy glowered at the prior and muttered curses under his breath.

The sheriff turned away angrily, but said nothing.

"You are a quarrelsome man," the abbot said to the prior, his heavy face shaking with anger. He pounded his fist on the table. "I want to eat. Where is my cellarer?"

"My lord abbot," the prior said and gestured to Lady Anne. "You have yet to hear this good woman, who has been waiting patiently. The Lady Anne of Havelond."

"Of Havelond?" Sir Guy said with a low snort. "I think not."

The abbot looked up as if he hadn't already seen Anne. "What do you want?"

Lady Anne stepped forward and curtsied. "God save you, my lord abbot. I have come to seek justice."

"What is your complaint?" the abbot asked.

Lady Anne explained about her husband's service in Scotland to King Henry, how he was taken captive and held for ransom, and how, now that the ransom had been paid, Sir Reynauld of Prestbury would not relinquish their lands. "Where is your husband?" the abbot asked, looking around the room. "I cannot address this case unless your husband comes to me in person."

"He would have come, my lord abbot, but he was severely beaten on his journey from Scotland." She looked down at her clasped hands and said, "There is evidence enough to believe Sir Reynauld was responsible for the attack."

Sir Guy rose to his feet. "This is a spurious accusation! What evidence?"

"I shall present it at the proper time," Lady Anne replied. "As it is, my lord abbot, it may be weeks before my husband is able to walk again."

"Then there is nothing to be done until he comes here himself," the abbot said.

Lady Anne took another step forward. "What am I to do, my lord? I fear for my life and the life of my husband. Sir Reynauld is prepared to commit any vile act to fix his hold upon my house and lands. I demand justice, my lord abbot."

The abbot gave a loud snort.

"Is there none to be found here?" Lady Anne asked.

Sir Guy hit the table with his hand. "You Saxons did not know the meaning of the word until we Normans taught it to you."

Lady Anne said calmly, "Sir Guy, the only thing the Normans taught us is that justice serves only the Normans."

The abbot jabbed a finger at the table. "Bennett must appear before me. *Here.* Until then, Sir Reynauld remains my steward at Havelond."

"My lord abbot, you force me to pursue justice by other means," Lady Anne proclaimed.

"Pray tell, what means are those?" Sir Guy asked. "You are cousin to the outlaw Robin Hood, are you not? Do you seek his aid? Do you know where he is even now? Perhaps the lord sheriff should arrest you as an accomplice."

"That would serve you and Sir Reynauld well," Lady Anne said. "'Tis a grievous feat to turn your victims into criminals." She held out her arms, pressing her wrists together. "Arrest me, then. Bind me. Then shall I present the evidence I have against Sir Reynauld, and the king's own justice will be forced to take action."

A nervous look came over the sheriff's face. "We must be calm," said the sheriff.

The abbot waved his hand to dismiss Lady Anne. "I am fatigued by this prattle. Bring your husband to me. In the meantime, you must pray that the Lord will provide," the abbot said wearily.

Lady Anne stepped to the very edge of the table. The abbot's narrow eyes opened ever so slightly. "I shall *pray*, my lord abbot, that our Lord will deal truly with wicked men who desire land that is not theirs, ever yearning to add acre to acre, grinding down the souls and bodies of the poor tenants who slave for them. For what? More wealth and more power to ruin and oppress those who cannot fight against their evil power! May the Lord provide an end to them, by whatever hand it may come."

The abbot fell back in his chair, his red face deepening to a dark purple. He sputtered, "Out, before I have you thrown out!"

Lady Anne gathered her skirt, turned, and marched out the door. Eve glanced back at the abbot, sure he was having a heart attack.

The prior seemed unconcerned and asked calmly, "Shall we hear the next case?"

Eve struggled to keep up with Lady Anne. The crowd in the hall, sensing her anger, parted like the Red Sea to allow her through.

"You were bold, my lady," Eve said as she came alongside her. "What evidence would you have given against Sir Reynauld?"

"I have none," Lady Anne said. "But they did not know that."

Nidd approached them in the courtyard, but Lady Anne did not break her stride to greet him.

"My Lady?" he asked, walking briskly to keep up with her.

"Robin spoke the truth," Lady Anne said to him. "There is no justice to be found here."

Andrew had been held captive overnight by Maurice and the two servants of Sir Alberic. They kept him at their sides at the inn for yet another night on stiff straw and hard wood. Now, as they stood outside of the prison waiting for Will Scarlet to be brought out by Captain Butcher, he was sandwiched between them. Walter of Larimore kept a heavy hand on his shoulder.

Voices could be heard from the other side of the stout iron-plated and rivet-studded gates. With creaking and jarring the great double doors swung open and twelve of the captain's guards marched out. Each had a steel cap on his head and wore a shirt of heavy mail. They held their swords high. In their midst was Will Scarlet, his hands held in front, bound with stout cords. His look was bold and his head held high as he walked. His expression changed only when he saw Andrew standing with his three adversaries.

Captain Butcher followed, barking commands for horses to be brought out.

"Why is the boy here?" the captain asked.

Maurice explained his conviction that Andrew was a spy for the outlaw's band.

Captain Butcher gave Andrew a malevolent look. "Put him on the horse with our other prisoner."

"I never learned how to ride a horse," Andrew said.

"You will learn," Maurice said. "Or die in the attempt."

The horses were trotted out. One was a scrawny nag. The guards heaved Will onto the nag, then Jenkins and Walter tossed Andrew in front of him. They gave Andrew the reins.

The captain insisted on a slow procession through town. Andrew assumed he was showing off his victory. The people gathered to watch as they passed, with eyes on Will Scarlet and Andrew and words whispered behind raised hands.

Andrew turned, speaking as softly as he could over his shoulder, "I have the Spanish knife under my tunic. I can cut you free."

"Not now, lad," Will said. "I will use it when the time is right."

They passed through the gate and set out on the open road. Maurice urged them to pick up their speed, swatting the rear of the old nag with his whip. The horse lurched forward, but only enough for Andrew to bounce uncomfortably.

As they rode, Andrew looked around at the countryside anxiously. He had hoped to see the outlaws rushing from the dark woods, but there was no sign of help anywhere. Peasants worked their lands, travelers walked with packs on their backs, and the occasional tradesman pulled a cart or urged a donkey along.

The warmth of the morning sun turned into an oppressive afternoon heat.

"Not far now," Will said.

As if on cue, the captain's guards spurred their horses and rode more quickly ahead, soon disappearing into a cloud of dust.

"Where are they going?" Andrew asked Will.

"Taking their positions," Will said. "Dare we hope that Master Robin is there to receive them?"

"What if he has gone to Nottingham to save you?" Andrew asked, remembering that Eve carried a message to Robin to do that very thing.

"Then we must make good use of that Spanish knife," Will said. "Pass it back. I will tuck it under the folds of my shirt."

Andrew waited until the eyes of their captors were elsewhere and then carefully slipped the knife into Will's hands.

They rode on, stopping only once for a few gulps of water and to stretch their legs. Andrew saw that three guards had stayed behind with them, hands on swords and eyes on the fields and woods around them.

Sometime late in the afternoon, Ravenswood came into view. It was little more than an inn with a handful of houses and shacks, fences for animals, and a few plowed fields. The inn sat at a crossroads, with a large empty field along side it. In the distance, Andrew saw the square tower of a church. The captain shouted to come off of the road and onto the barren field. They crossed to a lone oak tree standing in its center, the branches thick with green leaves. The guards dismounted.

The captain circled the nag and then pulled Andrew to the ground. His grip on the boy's arm was vice-like. "Try to run and an arrow will drop you before you take but a dozen steps," he said.

Will Scarlet was left on the nag.

Maurice sneered up at him. "No false moves by word of warning or deed, knave, or you will know suffering as never before."

Will Scarlet grunted.

Maurice summoned Jenkins to his side. "Go to the inn. Find Bennett."

"What if it is a trap?" Jenkins asked, worried.

"You will be the first to know," Maurice said with a low laugh. "Do you have a knife?"

"Aye," said Jenkins, touching his belt.

He gave Andrew a hard push toward the servant. "Take him with you," Maurice said. "Use him to protect yourself."

Jenkins grabbed Andrew by the scruff of the neck and pulled him across the uneven field, walking at first, then picking up the pace to a jog. "Pray, lad, that the outlaw is up to no tricks," Jenkins warned him.

They reached the front of the inn. Jenkins opened the door and stepped back, as if he expected an attack. Nothing happened. They stepped inside a large room with tables and chairs and a long counter, but no people.

A burly man came from a back room, wiping his hands on an apron. "Good day," he said.

Jenkins took Andrew's arm and led him to the counter. He leaned on the top of it and scowled at the innkeeper. "Where are the outlaws?" he demanded.

The innkeeper looked puzzled. "Outlaws?"

Jenkins pulled the knife from his belt and held it up. "Outlaws."

The innkeeper flinched and took a step back. "I serve all sorts in here," he stammered.

"Tell me, or you will feel this blade in your fat carcass." Jenkins's voice shook as he spoke, and Andrew realized he was afraid.

The innkeeper's eyes stayed on the knife. "The outlaw was here with some of his men, but received word that one of his own was to be hanged in Nottingham. They hastened away."

Andrew felt his heart sink. He had hoped that, somehow, Robin would know where Will Scarlet really was.

"Who is here now?" Jenkins asked.

"Myself," the innkeeper said. "Also a sick man lies upstairs in bed. He was terribly beaten and is near death."

"Is he alone? Who is with him?" Jenkins asked.

"The outlaw left an old woman to care for the man."
Beads of sweat had formed across the innkeeper's brow.
He wiped at them with a rag from his apron pocket.

"Take me to him," Jenkins said and tucked the knife
back into his belt.

The innkeeper waved for them to follow and led them
down a hall to a set of stairs near a back door. Jenkins
held Andrew in front of him, his grip hard on Andrew's
shoulders. They went up the stairs, each step creaking
loudly as they did. At the top, the innkeeper took them
down another hall, past an open door on the right, and
then stopped at the second.

"He is here," the innkeeper said softly.

"Open the door," Jenkins said.

The innkeeper obeyed, pushing the door open and
stepping back into the hall. The windowless room was
dark, apart from a lit candle on a bedside table. Andrew
saw a man lying in a bed. Sitting on a stool next to the
bed was a small figure in a hooded robe, leaning on the
edge of the mattress as if praying.

Jenkins took a step past Andrew into the room. His
hand drew the knife from his belt.

The innkeeper reached out and gently pulled Andrew
back. The floorboard groaned under their feet. Jenkins
turned in time to see them move and his sour expression
suddenly changed as he realized, too late, what he should
have known.

In a quick move, the figure on the stool was on his feet, a knife held ready. It was a man Andrew didn't recognize. Then the quilt was thrown aside and the sick man—Robin Hood himself—came off of the bed with a laugh.

Jenkins lifted his knife, but the innkeeper now had a knife of his own and held it against Jenkins's neck. Robin caught hold of Jenkins's wrist and twisted until Jenkins fell to his knees and dropped the knife. "Mercy! Have mercy!" Jenkins said through clenched teeth.

Robin picked up the knife and handed it to the innkeeper. "With gratitude," he said.

The innkeeper nodded, then quickly retreated down the hall to the stairs.

"How many of you are there?" Robin asked Jenkins.

"Only three," Jenkins said. "Captain Butcher, Master Maurice, and myself."

"He is lying," Andrew said. "The Captain brought a dozen guards with him, maybe more."

Robin gave a disappointed look at Jenkins. "What is your name?"

"Jenkins."

"I am the one they call Robin Hood, and this is Much the Miller's Son," Robin said cordially. Much nodded.

Jenkins looked puzzled by the introduction.

"Today you will be sorry you chose to serve the wrong master." He gave Jenkins a stunning blow on the side of the head with the hilt of his knife.

Jenkins fell, dazed, to one side, but Much's hands were on him, dragging him onto the bed. Rope seemed to come from nowhere as Much bound Jenkins's hands and feet.

Robin turned to Andrew. "What about you, lad? Are you hurt?"

"Saddle sore," he said.

Robin chuckled. "And Will Scarlet? Unharmed?"

"They have knocked him around, but he is tough," Andrew said. "How did you know we weren't in Nottingham?"

"Thanks be to God for men with fast legs," Robin said. "Where are they keeping Will now?"

"Under the tree in the middle of the field."

"So, they will see us coming, should we attack. Though we are positioned better than they know," Robin said. He bowed down to face Andrew. "I would not have you in harm's way again, lad, but I have need of your help."

"I will do whatever you want," Andrew said.

Andrew crossed the field alone. He could see Maurice and the captain pacing under the tall oak. They were watching him, the guards standing ready behind them. Will Scarlet was still on the horse but, as Andrew came closer, he saw that they'd put a noose around his neck and stretched it over a branch of the tree.

The captain drew his sword as Andrew approached. "Where is Jenkins?" he demanded.

Andrew swallowed hard, trying not to sound nervous. "At the inn. He wants you to come to see Bennett."

Maurice asked, "The outlaw left the man unguarded?"

"There was a guard," Andrew explained, "but Jenkins took care of him."

"What of the outlaw?" the captain asked. "Has he been here?"

"The innkeeper said Robin Hood and his men went to Nottingham to save Will Scarlet," Andrew replied. He looked at Will Scarlett, who gazed back at him with a blank expression.

Maurice gave a proud smile. "This is good news. I shall have Bennett and you will capture the outlaw when he rushes back from Nottingham."

"It is a trap," Captain Butcher said. In a quick move, he grabbed Andrew, drawing him close. "Is it a trap? Is the outlaw at the inn?"

Andrew acted surprised, which wasn't hard to do. He stammered, "Yes. Robin Hood is inside."

The captain snorted at Maurice, who turned red.

Andrew continued, "Robin wants you to know that you are surrounded by his men, though you cannot see them. He will strike a bargain with you: Jenkins for Will Scarlet."

"Let him kill Jenkins," Maurice said. "It was his incompetence that brought us to this trouble."

The captain sheathed his sword. "Does the scoundrel expect us to bring Will Scarlet to him?"

"He will meet you in front of the inn to make the exchange," Andrew said.

The captain shook his head. "He will have the advantage there. The rogue and his men must be drawn out."

"How? Invite them to make the exchange in the middle of the field?" Maurice asked.

The captain scowled at Maurice. "There will be no exchange, you fool. We must prepare for battle."

Maurice looked stunned. "A battle?"

"I did not come this far to trade men with an outlaw I mean to capture," the captain snarled. "We will draw him and his hidden bandits out into the clear."

"By what means?"

The captain pointed to Will on the horse. "By hanging this brigand."

Will turned to the captain but said nothing.

Andrew cried out, "No!"

The captain gave a look to one of his guards, who took hold of Andrew and dragged him over to the side of the nag. "Move and I have orders to kill you," the guard snarled.

Andrew looked up at Will. The noose was fixed tight around his neck, the rope disappearing into the foliage of the tree, then dropping down again. His eye went to Will's hands. He hoped Will had secretly used the Spanish knife to cut the cords, but they were still there.

The captain gave orders to another guard. "Ride to the inn. Tell the outlaw to surrender or I will hang his friend. If he doubts me, then let him but watch from his hiding place."

The guard mounted his horse and sped across the field. He dismounted at the front door of the inn. Andrew saw Robin come out to greet the guard. They spoke for a moment and the guard climbed upon the horse and rode back.

"What does the robber say?" the captain called out.

"He sends this message: 'Release Will Scarlet and the boy or you and all with you will suffer grievous harm, even to the pain of death,'" the guard said.

"So be it," the captain said and, taking out his sword, strode over to the nag. He lifted the sword and turned the flat side to strike the flank of the horse.

Andrew and Will exchanged glances. With a voice of stone, Will said, "A battle with great bloodshed is needless. If I must die, grant me this much: give me a sword and let me be unbound to fight with you and your men until I lie dead on the ground."

Captain Butcher looked at him scornfully. "A thieving varlet does not deserve to die so honorably. You will hang, as will the rest of your cutthroat comrades."

Maurice's face bunched up with worry, and he called out, "Give them a moment to change their minds."

The captain snorted. "I shall not." He brought the flat of the sword down with a loud slap onto the back end of the horse.

The horse bolted forward, and Will Scarlet slid off the back. Andrew was prepared to rush forward to grab Will's legs, with a vain hope of holding him up so he wouldn't hang. The guard gripped him tighter.

"Stop!" Andrew cried out.

Will hung for only a few seconds, then suddenly jerked his hands apart, the cords flying aside. With both hands, he grabbed the rope above his head to alleviate its strangling hold. Then, like magic, Will seemed to fly up into the tree and disappear into its thick leaves.

"By the devil!" Captain Butcher shouted, lifting his sword and moving under the tree to look.

There was a buzz like the sound of a bee as a small black arrow flew down from somewhere in the tree, striking the captain on the top of his shoulder. He staggered back with a loud cry. The guards raced to him, pulling him from danger.

The guard holding Andrew pushed him away and left to see to his captain. Andrew fell at the thick base of the tree. Looking up, he saw Will on a high branch, cutting the noose from his neck. Next to him was Ket the Troll, with his small bow held up in his left hand and his right hand stringing one arrow after another and letting them fly.

Maurice and the guards scattered from under the tree, exposing themselves in the surrounding field. Arrows now flew from different directions, from both the inn and the distant woods. Andrew saw Robin Hood and

Much the Miller's Son running in their direction. The captain's guards turned this way and that, seeking cover but not sure which direction to go. "Haste, haste," cried one guard. "Away! Away!"

There was a *thud* next to Andrew as Will Scarlet dropped from the tree. He grasped the boy with both hands and tossed him up to Ket the Troll. "For safekeeping," he said and sprinted toward Captain Butcher with his Spanish knife drawn.

"Hello, lad," Ket said in his usual low, mournful voice.

Andrew positioned himself on a thick branch and strained to see what was happening below. A guard and Will Scarlet, both with knives at the ready, circled one another.

More guards, with swords held high, erupted from their hiding places in the forest, on horseback and on foot.

Andrew saw it all, feeling as if he'd slipped into a nightmare. Swords and knives were brandished, clashing loudly as they struck one another. Spears were thrown, arrows buzzed, men struggled in hand-to-hand combat. Fear surged through Andrew's body. *This is nothing like the movies*, he thought. Then came a wave of adrenaline that sharpened his focus and heightened his sense of everyone's movements, almost as if in slow motion.

Robin Hood was closer to the tree now, clashing swords with a guard. Captain Butcher emerged from somewhere out of Andrew's view, clutching his sword. He circled behind Robin, whose attention was on the guard. Andrew knew that, unless someone did something, the captain would strike Robin down. Andrew shouted, but his voice disappeared in the noise below.

Andrew turned to Ket the Troll, who had moved to another branch to release his black arrows in another direction.

Andrew half-scrambled, half-fell, from branch to branch to the ground below. The captain was coming up behind Robin, his sword ready for a terrible thrust. Andrew knew he had to do something and, looking around, saw a stone the size of his fist on the ground. He whispered, "God help me," and, in one swift move, snatched up the stone and threw it as hard as he could at the captain.

The stone curved in the air—better than any curve-ball Andrew had ever thrown—and hit Captain Butcher hard on the left temple. The man spun as his legs went limp. He fell in a heap behind the outlaw.

The sudden distraction of the fallen captain allowed Robin to dispense with the guard in front of him. He swung around to the fallen captain, looked puzzled, then saw Andrew standing by the tree. A quick nod of thanks and Robin dashed into the battle again.

Andrew pressed against the tree, worried he might be struck by an arrow or a swinging sword. The fight continued with a terrible ferocity on the field. Then, a single man broke away, running from the combat for the forest. It was Maurice.

"He is getting away!" Andrew shouted to no one in particular. Getting no response, Andrew ran after him.

Only after he had made it across the road and into the woods did Andrew wonder what he would do if he caught up to the man.

The sound of a horse's snort turned his attention to the right. Through the trees, Walter, Sir Alberic's other servant, was climbing onto a horse. A second horse came into view and Andrew knew how they would escape.

A twig snapped and Andrew turned in time to see Maurice reaching for him. He tried to dodge, but Maurice caught hold of his tunic and threw him to the ground. The man followed it with a hard kick to his side, knocking the wind out of him. Andrew doubled up, wheezing, trying to breathe as black spots formed in front of his eyes.

Maurice's hands were on him again, dragging him across the ground by his arm. A moment later, he was thrown onto a horse. Maurice climbed on behind him, whipping at the horse to move.

Andrew heard a sharp hiss, followed by a loud cry from Walter. The servant fell to the ground, a black arrow sticking from his chest.

Maurice spurred his horse into a gallop, then a full run through the trees.

Still straining to get air into his lungs, Andrew struggled to stay conscious and wondered if he'd ever get out of this world alive.

12

Havelond.

Andrew, who had recovered enough to watch where they were going and hope for a chance to escape, now saw the familiar grounds. It was near evening and the manor house was taking on an ominous darkness.

Maurice guided the horse along a side path to the courtyard and stable. He dismounted and barked commands for the "beggar boy" to be brought inside. The large man who'd grabbed Andrew when he'd first arrived now seized him again and hooked an arm around his waist. Andrew cried out as a sharp pain shot through his side where Maurice had kicked him. The thug was unconcerned and carried him into the manor.

Andrew was brought to a large dining hall. A massive rectangular table framed by a dozen chairs dominated the center. A wall-sized stone fireplace stood at the far end. Tall narrow windows lining another wall were propped open and fresh air wafted in.

Maurice was leaning over a side table, splashing water from a bowl onto his face.

The thug dropped Andrew onto a chair near the side table and lumbered out again. Andrew gingerly touched his side. He knew it was bruised but worried that Maurice's kick had damaged a rib.

Maurice lifted a pitcher and poured a drink into a tall silver cup. "You want some, I am sure," Maurice said.

"Yes please," Andrew said, realizing how thirsty he was.

With a cruel smile, Maurice drained the cup, then slammed it down with a contented "ah!" He didn't offer any water to Andrew.

A set of double doors at the head of the room opened. Sir Reynauld walked in with his son Everard and a man with a pointed face and narrow eyes that reminded Andrew of a rat. Maurice greeted them and only then did Andrew discover that the man was Sir Alberic.

Sir Alberic was taller than the other men, though his slumped shoulders curved his lean body slightly forward. He clasped his hands loosely in front of his chest, the thin fingers threaded into each other. He wore a long black robe that contrasted the pale skin on his rodent-like features.

"I am surprised you would greet me so cheerfully," Sir Alberic said to Maurice in a voice that matched his look, "since you have suffered to fail so miserably."

"Failed, Sir Alberic?"

"Where are my servants? Why have they not returned to me with news of Bennett?"

"Your servant Walter is dead," Maurice reported. "I know not what has become of Jenkins. It was their failure you should consider, not mine." He gave Sir Alberic a sharp look. "I would have thought a man of your stature would have had more competent servants to do his bidding."

Sir Alberic's lips pulled back into a smile that also served as a sneer.

"Mind your tongue," Sir Reynauld said to his son. "Where, then, is Bennett?"

"He is missing," Maurice replied.

"Perhaps you should tell us all that happened after your arrival in Nottingham," Sir Alberic said.

Andrew listened as Maurice told his tale, which mixed a little fact with a lot of fiction. He claimed it was Captain Butcher who came up with the foolish scheme to travel to Ravenswood to capture Robin Hood, kill Bennett to please Sir Reynauld, and find Reuben to gain favor with Sir Alberic. "I was a reluctant participant," Maurice concluded and explained how the scheme had gone wrong after they were ambushed by the outlaws.

Sir Alberic paced calmly as he listened, his hands rubbing together.

Sir Reynauld's face contorted with rage. "Fools to a man! And you, my son, were the biggest of them all."

Maurice reeled back, as if struck. He glared at his father, but did not speak.

Everard gave an apologetic look to his brother. He turned to his father and asked, "What are we to do now?"

"The abbot and Sir Guy of Gisborne have given us additional time by rebuffing the Lady Anne," Sir Reynauld said. "She may not make a claim against us unless Bennett himself appears before the abbot in York. We may yet find him before that happens."

"Their aid allows you more time in Havelond, but it does not help me with Reuben of Stamford," Sir Alberic said with a loud sniff. "Reuben may yet still demand the money he expects from me. The Jew must be found."

"No doubt the outlaw is hiding the two of them," said Sir Reynauld.

"Now you see why I have brought the boy," Maurice said.

With that, all eyes in the room turned to Andrew.

Sir Alberic stepped to the chair and leaned over Andrew, his hands still clasped in front of him. "Speak, young beggar. What reward would satisfy you if you would tell us how to find Reuben of Stamford and Bennett?" Sir Alberic's beady eyes locked onto Andrew's.

At that moment, Andrew realized that Sir Alberic reminded him more of a praying mantis than a rat. "Sir, I do not know where they are," he said. "I am not from these parts. Free me now to walk the forest and I would be completely lost within mere minutes."

The men looked at one another.

"I will beat it out of him," Sir Reynauld said.

He had taken only two steps when, suddenly, Andrew heard a familiar buzz and a black arrow slammed into the top of the dining table, narrowly missing the man.

The men were startled, throwing themselves to one side and the other while craning to see from where the arrow had come.

"Are we under attack?" Everard cried out from behind a chair.

"I know that black arrow," Maurice said, half-hidden under the table. "'Tis one of Robin Hood's men."

Sir Alberic had pressed himself against the wall next to Andrew. He glanced at the window, then grabbed at the arrow. It was firmly embedded in the wooden table-top. He knelt and peered close. "A parchment is tied to the shaft."

Sir Reynauld snatched up a long pole that had been leaning against the wall between the windows. Positioning himself out of harm's way, he used the pole to close the thick wooden shutters. He dropped the pole and walked with renewed confidence to the arrow. The others also relaxed. Sir Reynauld undid the thin string that held the roll of parchment in place.

"*Sir Reynauld of Prestbury and Sir Alberic de Wisgar,*" he read aloud, "*your debts are now due. Depart Havelond by daybreak with all that is yours. Heed this warning or suffer the pain of your treachery.*"

Everard went pale. "The outlaws know you are here, Sir Alberic."

Sir Reynauld slammed a fist against the table. "Who is that lawless wretch to dictate to us?"

"What shall we do?" asked Everard.

His father looked at him with contempt. "You mew like a coward," he said. "Call the men-at-arms. Command them to guard every corner of this manor."

"You would have them lay siege to us?" Maurice asked.

"I do not believe the outlaw has enough men to entrap us here," he said. "However, I would have you and Everard depart with great speed to Prestbury to summon our allies."

"Now?" Everard asked. "To travel by night will lay us open to ambush by the outlaw's cutthroats."

"Only if you tarry."

Everard came closer to his father. "We cannot make the journey there and return before dawn," he said. "Father, you do not know the strength of the outlaw. If you are not seen departing by the morning, he will attack."

"I do not fear the scoundrel as you do," Sir Reynauld said firmly. "Do as I say!"

Everard bowed and left the room. Maurice lingered, looking as if he wanted to say something, but changed his mind. He glanced at Andrew. "What about the boy?"

"Leave him to us," said Sir Reynauld.

Maurice turned on his heels and walked out.

Sir Reynauld went to the door and pulled at a long cord. "Sir Alberic, 'tis safer for you to stay here than to attempt to journey home. Let us see to supper."

Sir Alberic gave a bow of gratitude. "It would seem we must now fight the outlaw together."

The two men turned their attention to Andrew again.

"Pray tell, what shall we do with you?" Sir Alberic asked.

"Give me a drink of water and set me free?" Andrew suggested.

Sir Alberic leered at him. "You have the saucy tongue of your master," he said.

Andrew shrugged.

"We shall cure you of that," Sir Alberic said.

Andrew was locked in a closet with no food nor drink nor light, save a thin gray line that shone from under the door. Once his eyes adjusted, he saw shelves lining one wall. He felt plates and pitchers on one. He didn't find any food or water. His fingers touched rough blankets on another shelf. He grabbed them and spread them on the floor as a bed. With nothing better to do, he lay down with his head close to the crack under the door, hoping for a clue about what was happening. He prayed for someone to rescue him.

His bruised side ached no matter which position he took. Eventually, from the sheer exhaustion caused by the long day, he fell asleep. How long he slept, he didn't know, but he woke up to the same foreboding darkness. His mouth was dry. He had trouble swallowing. His head began to hurt. A wave of nausea hit his stomach.

I'm dehydrated, he thought.

Performing the Sign of the Cross, he prayed, "Dear God, please provide me with water."

Lying down again, he closed his eyes and fell into a fitful half-asleep/half-awake state, like a fever-dream. He came out of it when a sound—he didn't know what it was—caused him to sit up. He listened. A low rumbling of thunder came, followed quickly by a torrent of rain that fell heavy against the house.

If only there was a window, he thought. *I could reach out for a handful of water.*

He lay back down, praying again for God to help him. He hadn't finished the prayer when a drop of water hit him on the forehead. Then another. And another.

A leak in the roof!

He pushed himself up a few inches and opened his mouth. A drop of water hit his tongue. He held his position as more drops fell, giving him relief.

Thank you, God, he thought, as more drops came.

He had an idea and placed a pitcher from the shelf where his head had been. The drops splashed inside, spraying him and the blankets.

"You can stop now," he said to God after he'd filled that pitcher and started another.

He curled up in a ball away from the leak and fell asleep feeling better than he had for hours.

A gentle scratching sound woke him up the next time.

Rats, he thought. Then he realized the sound was coming from the lock on the door. He crawled over and listened. Someone was turning a key in the lock. There was a gentle click and the door slowly opened.

"Andrew?" a low and mournful voice said.

"Ket?" whispered Andrew. "Ket the Troll?"

"Aye," he said. "We must move quickly. The wicked knights intend to deliver your dead body to Master Robin to prove they do not fear him."

Andrew's mouth went dry. His hand bumped against the pitcher of rainwater. He drank some of it but felt a new wave of nausea.

"They are coming for you now. Follow me," Ket said.

Andrew stood up, his legs cramping, and entered the dark hallway with Ket. The troll closed the closet door and locked it again.

Heavy footsteps sounded from somewhere down the hall. Ket tugged at Andrew's sleeve and together they went down a hall in the opposite direction of the noise. They reached the double doors of the dining hall and slipped in.

"How will we get out?" Andrew asked.

"By going up," Ket said. He went to a tall hutch in the far corner of the room and climbed the shelves to the very top. He reached a hand down to Andrew. Andrew caught it and climbed as Ket pulled with greater strength than Andrew imagined.

"Further on," Ket said, and now leapt up, grabbing a crossbeam on the ceiling. He swung up and, as before, reached down for Andrew, who took his hand again. And so it went until Ket and Andrew were high in the rafters, crawling along the beams to the far end.

"You did not shoot the black arrow through the window, did you? You shot it from up here," Andrew said.

"Near enough to the open window so they would think it came from outside."

"How will we get out?" Andrew asked, thinking of the narrow windows.

"'Tis the only way," the troll replied. "You must squeeze through as I did."

As the two crept along the crossbeam, the doors below were thrown open. Ket signaled for Andrew to stop.

The large servant that had manhandled Andrew earlier entered with a lamp.

"What do you mean, 'the closet was empty'?" Sir Reynauld shouted, coming in behind the servant. "Dullard! Did you forget to lock the door?"

"No, my lord," the servant said. "He was there most of the night. He used blankets as a bed and collected rainwater to drink. Someone from outside must have taken the key from the hook and set him free."

"Raise the alarm," Sir Reynauld thundered. "Search the house. Find that boy!"

The servant started through the door.

"Leave the lamp!" Sir Reynauld barked.

The servant put the lamp on the table and hurried out.

Sir Reynauld put both hands on the table and leaned forward, groaning loudly.

"Is it time for breakfast?" Sir Alberic asked casually as he walked in. He was fully dressed.

"Someone freed the boy."

"Pity," he said, his hands coming up and clasping in their familiar position. "How did the boy escape?"

"The clumsiness of my servant, no doubt," Sir Reynauld said. "He shall pay dearly for his mistake."

A maidservant came in, still wearing a dressing gown and looking terrified. "My lord?" she asked.

"Food," Sir Reynauld commanded.

The maidservant bowed and rushed out.

The two knights lit candles around the room, though a gray light was creeping across the windows. They sat at the table in silence.

Sir Alberic looked up at the window. "The outlaw demanded that we leave Havelond by sunrise."

"Let the outlaw demand what he will. I am not afraid of him." Sir Reynauld gazed at Sir Alberic. "Are you? Do you intend to repay the Jew?"

Sir Alberic gave a light laugh. "Let him come to collect."

A flurry of servants arrived with trays covered with plates of food and goblets. Without a word, Sir Reynauld began to eat. Sir Alberic waited until the servants left again, then delicately nibbled at his food.

Andrew's mouth watered. He couldn't remember the last time he'd eaten. He looked at Ket, who sat perfectly still with his eyes on the scene below. He lifted his head and turned it slightly as if listening to something. Andrew listened but couldn't hear anything, apart from the sounds of the men eating below.

Suddenly, shouts erupted from somewhere in the house, then came the sound of feet pounding hard in the hall. Everard appeared in the doorway.

"Father!" he cried out. "Thank God you are not dead."

He was soaked from head to foot. His hair was matted against his skull and his face was streaked with mud.

Sir Reynauld stood up. "Dead! Whatever are you talking about? What has happened?"

Everard dropped into a chair, slouching wearily. "Prestbury House has been burned to the ground." He covered his face with his hands and sobbed.

Andrew looked at Ket. Ket gave a slight nod, then turned his attention to the scene below.

Sir Reynauld snapped his fingers at a servant standing in the corner. "Bring him a cup of ale."

The servant did as he was told.

Everard drank quickly and said, "The outlaws caught us as we reached the grounds of Prestbury. We fought them. Maurice most valiantly of all."

Sir Reynauld clutched a fist to his chest. "Where is Maurice now?"

"Captured, my lord. The outlaws have stolen him away into the forest." Everard pounded the cup on the table. The servant fumbled to pour him another drink.

"How is it that you are unscathed?" Sir Alberic asked.

"The outlaws spared me so I would deliver a message to you." The young man drained the cup again.

"What message?"

"We must depart Havelond *now*, taking only what we can carry, knowing we will never return."

Sir Reynauld snorted. "If they have destroyed our home, where do they expect us to go?"

"To Thornbridge," his son said. "They have demanded that we come to Thornbridge, with Sir Alberic. They said to obey and we may see Maurice yet alive."

"I am to go to Thornbridge?" Sir Alberic asked. "For what purpose?"

"To face your accusers," said Everard.

"What accusers?" asked Sir Alberic.

"Reuben of Stamford will be there."

"The brazenness! The effrontery!" Sir Reynauld roared. "I will not suffer the threats of that swine!"

Everard reached out and caught his father's hand. "My lord father, we must do as they say. I fear for the life of Maurice. I fear for all of our lives. Let us do as they say: depart with what we have, the flesh on our bones if nothing else. I beg you. Had you seen the devastation that was once our home, you would not doubt them."

Sir Reynauld pulled his hand away. "You are like the daughter I never had," he said. "Let them come here. See if they have the will or men to drive us out."

"We have not the men! Maurice and I never reached our allies!" Everard cried. "Be wise, Father. This manor house was not built to withstand a siege."

"'Tis true," Sir Alberic said with a sigh. He dabbed at his mouth with a napkin and threw it onto the plate. "We must go to Thornbridge."

"What?" Sir Reynauld shouted.

"I will remind you again, Father, that the life of your oldest son depends upon our going," Everard said.

"Hear me," Sir Alberic said. "I shall send a servant to York to rally the sheriff and all of the forces he can muster. They will surround the outlaws at Thornbridge. Not only will you keep Havelond, but I shall be rid of Reuben."

"If you are resolute to fight, then I beg you to send a message to Wrangby Castle for Sir Guy and the knights there to give us aid!" Everard said.

"Coward!" Sir Reynaud suddenly struck his son with the palm of his hand. The slap was so hard, and the sound so sharp, that Andrew recoiled and his hand stirred dust from the top of the beam. Ket grabbed his shoulder to steady him. Alarmed, Andrew watched specks of dust float downward toward Sir Alberic, who was still seated at the table.

"You are an embarrassment to me," Sir Reynauld snarled. "We shall show Sir Guy of Gisborne and all the knights of the realm our true power. All will know our mettle when we deliver the outlaw's head by our own strength."

Everard stood, glowered at his father, and stormed out of the room.

Sir Reynauld gave a contemptuous look to Sir Alberic, who turned just as the dust settled on the table near his plate.

"We must depart," Sir Reynauld said and marched out.

A moment later, Sir Alberic stood up and finished the last of his drink. He grimaced and smacked his lips as if he'd tasted something he didn't like. He put the cup down and sauntered out.

Ket moved toward the far wall. Andrew crawled behind him, still wishing he could grab a few of the leftovers from the plates below. Ket stopped again and looked down.

A maidservant entered the room and stacked the plates onto a tray. Then she turned and went to the window. Using the long pole, she unlatched and pushed open the heavy shutters. A cool morning breeze blew in and the yellow glow of sunrise touched the small panes of glass.

The maidservant stopped where she was and tilted her head up. She looked directly at Ket and Andrew. "God be with you," she said and took the tray from the room.

"We must hurry," Ket said and hurried forward.

The world seemed to glisten in the morning light as Andrew and Ket sprinted along the outer wall to the closest edge of the forest. Andrew braced himself for the sudden shouts from guards standing watch, but all was silent.

They moved into the trees and seemed to circle Havelond. Andrew had the sense that they were near the cave he'd first come through and wondered what he'd find if he went there now.

Ket stopped and said, "I shall intercept the servant bearing the message to Sir Alberic's men in York."

"What about me?"

"The way to Thornbridge is lined with forest," Ket said. "You must follow Sir Reynauld and Sir Alberic, lest they change their plans."

"What good will that do?" Andrew asked, thinking that he had no way to signal anyone if anything changed.

"Master Robin's men will be watching in the woods. Should you sense any danger, signal them with this whistle."

Ket cupped his hands around his mouth and whistled one long note, followed by two short ones. To Andrew's ear, it sounded like another bird call. "Now you."

Andrew tried the same signal, though it didn't sound as good as Ket's.

"That will do," Ket said and patted Andrew on the back. He was off, sprinting through the trees until he seemed to blend in to the forest itself.

Drops of water fell from the leaves above Andrew's head. He tilted his head back and let the drops fall into his mouth. Then he made his way toward the clearing that separated the forest from Havelond Manor.

A movement just ahead made him stop. He peered through the trees and saw Everard walking along the edge of the trees. Andrew crept closer to see what he was up to.

The young man hung his head, his hands clasped behind his back. He seemed lost in his thoughts as he strolled along the field, parallel to the house.

Andrew climbed the nearest tree, crawling along the branches, as he'd done before with Eve, leaping quietly from tree to tree, the leaves shivering only slightly as he did. *I'm getting pretty good at this*, he thought. He kept Everard in sight, allowing him to walk several yards ahead.

Everard reached a point where, to continue on, he would have gone around to the front of the house. Instead, he stopped. Andrew couldn't see why and carefully crawled along a branch to find a better vantage point. At the end of that branch, he reached for another and slipped. He lost balance and, with a lot of unhelpful grabbing and clawing, fell to a branch below, then bounced to one side into open air and soon found himself with his back flat against the ground.

If the kick to his side from Maurice hadn't fractured a rib, then his fall might have done the trick. With great effort, he rolled onto his hands and knees.

Everard was sitting on a tree stump, his elbows on his knees, his head still hung low. He looked over at Andrew with a forlorn expression. "Why are you here? Why have you not run to freedom?"

"That is a good question," Andrew said, groaning. He climbed to his feet and brushed himself off. His bruised side throbbed with a dull ache.

Everard sighed. "This is folly," he said. His eyes were red and the side of his face swollen where his father had struck him.

Across the field, servants led horses out from the stable. Soon, a cart followed. Then another. Everything was being moved to the front of the manor.

Everard turned to Andrew again. "Do you have a brother?"

"Yes," he replied.

"Would you not do all in your power to save him if his life were in danger?"

"Not when he uses my stuff without asking," Andrew said, adding a chuckle to show he was joking.

Everard didn't notice. "I must find the outlaw and plead for my brother's life."

Andrew was surprised.

"Will you lead me to the outlaw?" Everard asked.

"You will find Robin at Thornbridge," Andrew said.

"I must speak with him *before* the meeting with my father. Otherwise, I fear there will be no time for sensible talk," Everard said. He stood up and faced Andrew. "Will you lead me to him?"

Andrew shook his head. "I do not know where he is."

"Surely, if we walk in the direction of Thornbridge, you have the means to signal the outlaw or one of his men. I hear they are everywhere."

Andrew thought of the whistle Ket had taught him. "Yes, but . . . how do I know you are not part of a trap?"

Everard spread his arms wide. "I go with no more than what you see here, without the benefit of a sword or my father or any other aid. You, beggar boy, are the only aid I have in the world."

Andrew gazed at him. What was he supposed to do? Ket's orders were to follow Sir Reynauld, not guide one of his sons to Robin Hood. *But*, he reasoned, *if Everard is able to talk to Robin Hood and stop a battle, then it has to be worth it.*

"My family is doomed unless I intercede," Everard said.

Andrew made up his mind. "If you know the way to Thornbridge, I will try to send a message to Robin Hood."

"God bless you, boy," Everard said, relieved, and turned away from the manor. Together they went into the woods.

Everard followed the same path through the woods that Eve and Andrew had taken when they followed Lady Anne. This time, Everard didn't join the road, but veered off in a different direction that took them around the other side of Lady Anne's cottage. "She deserved better," he said as they passed and picked up his pace.

Andrew asked, "Why did you make her move there?"

"My father and I fell in love with Havelond. My brother fell in love with Lady Anne," Everard said. "Alas, she did not feel the same for him."

"She was married," Andrew reminded him.

Everard frowned. "He did not care. He wanted her. That was enough."

"Your family takes whatever it wants," Andrew said.

Everard eyed him, then nodded. "Aye. 'Tis a great fault that infects us, a deep pride that drives us to possess what we covet."

They walked on in silence. Andrew stayed watchful, staying at least an arm's length away from the young man, never losing his worry that Everard was using him to set a trap for Robin. His instincts seemed sharp, sharper than he'd ever known before. He saw things he normally wouldn't notice: a bird with speckled brown wings perched upon a branch; a hare moving cautiously through the brush; the deep earthy smell of the forest; the hint of smoke from a distant fire. Even the trees that had all looked the same before now took on distinctive characteristics. He was aware of their different shapes and sizes, the way the branches reached out, the shapes of their leaves. The world seemed more alive to him, and he was more alive within it.

With that feeling came another: they were being watched. Andrew was sure he saw a figure just behind a tree in one direction, and another figure crouching on a branch in a tree the other.

"The Thorn Bridge is but a mile ahead," Everard said.

"Is it an actual bridge?" asked Andrew.

"What else would it be?" Everard put to him.

"I thought it was just a name," Andrew said, thinking of his own time and how often streets and neighborhoods were named things that had nothing to do with what or where they were. "Is it made of thorns?"

"'Tis a bridge that sits on the Thorn River," Everard said.

"Makes sense," Andrew said and, without explaining, cupped his hands around his mouth and whistled loudly one long note and two short ones.

Everard stopped and looked at him, startled.

The voice of a boy came from only a few feet away to their left. "We have been wondering if you would signal, Friend of the Waif," he said, as he came out from behind an oak tree.

"Greetings," Andrew said, surprised to be looking at a boy younger than himself, dressed in the clothes of an outlaw, complete with a long knife on his belt. He held a bow in one hand and reached back to a quiver of short arrows slung on his back.

Everard looked him over and said, "Is the outlaw's band made up entirely of boys?"

"I am Gilbert of the White Hand," the boy said, notching an arrow into the bow string. "I am the nephew of Will Scarlet, the man your brother attempted to hang."

Everard held up his hands in surrender.

"He has come to beg Robin Hood for his brother's life," Andrew said.

"Alone?" another voice said from behind them.

Everard and Andrew turned. A tall man Andrew hadn't met stood with a spear ready to be thrown.

"We are alone," said Andrew.

"Follow me," Gilbert said.

They walked deeper into the woods, with Gilbert occasionally glancing back at them. The tall man with the spear stayed several yards behind them.

"The Thorn Bridge is that way," Everard said, pointing to the right.

"We are not going to the Thorn Bridge," Gilbert said, and walked to the left.

They arrived at a meadow. In the center, standing with his hands on his hips as if he'd been waiting for them, was Robin Hood. He took off his hat and gave them a low bow. "Hail, Everard, son of Sir Reynauld of Prestbury."

"Greetings to you, Robin of Barnsdale and the Outwoods, Robert of Locksley, and all other names and lands you claim as your own," Everard said, also bowing.

"The Greenwood is the only land I call home," Robin said. He came alongside Andrew and placed a firm hand on his shoulder. "You have done well, lad."

Andrew felt a blush of pride creep into his cheeks.

"Where is my brother?" Everard insisted.

"Are you demanding to know?" Robin said, glaring at the man. "Hardly the tone of one who has come to beg."

Everard bristled. "*Beg*, outlaw?"

Andrew looked at him with surprise. What had happened to the red-eyed man he saw sitting on a tree stump? Where was the man who was ready to plead for his brother's life?

Robin suddenly laughed. "You truly are the son of your father. The walk from Havelond has rekindled your pride and stiffened your neck."

"It was not the walk," Everard said, speaking through gritted teeth. "It is standing face to face with a man I know to be a thief and a murderer."

Robin stepped back from Everard, giving him a steely look. "If I am a thief or a murderer, then you may thank men like yourself for having made me so, as I take only to give back to others in need, or kill only to spare the lives of those who cannot defend themselves. You, son of Sir Reynauld, rob and kill for your own good pleasure."

Andrew saw Everard's fists clench.

Robin saw it as well and cried, "By the rood! I have consented to meet you in good faith, believing you to be of a character apart from your kin. Before Our Lady, the Mother of Our Lord, I vowed to hear you as an act of peace. Was I mistaken?" He raised a hand and several men emerged from different parts of the forest surrounding them.

Everard turned, his hand going to his belt to find a knife that was not there. "Scoundrel, wicked and foul—"

"I am done with you, Everard. You will be led away to join your father's caravan, come what may," Robin said.

Andrew felt anger burn like coals through his body. He couldn't stand it anymore. "Stop!" he suddenly shouted.

Surprised, both Robin and Everard looked at him.

"You are worse than kids on a playground," he said, his voice full of scorn. He stepped up to Everard. "What are you doing? You came here to save your brother's life! You said you wanted to stop this battle!"

Everard stood, stunned.

Andrew continued, "Remember what you said about pride? Are you going to let it kill your brother today? Are you really like your father after all?"

Everard reached up and gently touched the place on his face where he'd been slapped by his father. His expression, which had grown hard while talking to Robin, now softened. "Aye," he said to Andrew. "'Tis a family curse that comes upon me like a fever."

"'Tis the curse of Adam and it may bring us all to a sorrowful end," Robin said, his tone also softening. "You have spoken wisely, lad. Young Everard, let us begin anew."

Everard unexpectedly knelt down on one knee in front of the outlaw. "The boy is right, noble outlaw. I have come to beg for my brother's life and to secure peace so that others will not die from an act of pure vanity."

Robin took the young man's arms and guided him to his feet. "Rise, Everard. You are worthy to be heard. Let us pray you will prevail upon your father to subdue his pride this day. Come! I shall take you to your brother, who is recovering from his wounds."

"Wounds?"

"Mere scratches, of little concern. 'Tis his broken leg that troubled us."

"How, pray tell, was his leg broken?" Everard asked.

"A foolish attempt to escape in a part of the forest he did not know. He spurred the horse to hurdle a fallen tree and was thrown off. Our physician assures us of his recovery, thanks be to God. See for yourself."

"With gratitude," Everard said.

The two men walked off across the meadow, with the tall man following, spear in hand.

Andrew turned, unsure of where to go, and saw Gilbert waiting nearby. "Gilbert, where is Eve?"

Gilbert looked unsure. "Eve?"

"Evangeline, the Waif of the Woods," Andrew corrected himself.

Gilbert's face lit up. "This way."

The young boy led Andrew back into the forest. A path took them to a cabin partially obscured by dense trees. A guard, whom Gilbert called Thomas of Helmsdale, stood watch. He gave the door a sharp knock and moved aside. The door opened. Eve was coming out with a silver pitcher in her hand.

"Andrew!" she shrieked and, before Andrew could react, dropped the pitcher and gave him a hug. Then, just as suddenly, she pushed back, her face red.

Gilbert and Thomas turned away, but Andrew saw that they were laughing.

Eve stammered, "I am sorry. I have been worried about you."

"Me too," he said, his cheeks burning.

They looked at each other, neither one knowing what to say next.

Eve bent down and picked up the silver pitcher. "Water," she said. "I am getting water for Reuben and Ruth. You can help."

They used the short walk to a stream to tell briefly what had happened since they parted ways in Nottingham, leading to this final meeting in Thornbridge.

"Reuben and Ruth are afraid," Eve admitted. "They believe Sir Alberic is going to trick Robin and attack them. They say he is a son of the devil."

Andrew nodded. "He is creepy. He does this thing with his hands that makes him look like a praying mantis."

The stream cut through the woods between wall-like ridges of trees and brush. They found their footing down a gentle slope that put them on a bank where a small waterfall, created by a natural formation of rocks, formed a pool. Eve knelt down and filled the pitcher.

Andrew stooped to splash water onto his face, head, and neck. It was so refreshing that he decided it wasn't enough and fell into the pool.

Eve screamed with laughter.

The pool was only a few feet deep. Andrew splashed, went under, and emerged again closer to the waterfall.

"Silly boy," Eve called to him.

The sound of the splashing water roared nearby.

Eve shouted and gestured, "Your belt! Your knife will get rusty."

Andrew hadn't thought of that. A small clump of bushes sat within arm's reach by the waterfall. He undid his belt and tucked it, with the knife, underneath. He dropped into the pool again and rolled to let the water clean off the day's dust and dirt.

The ripples in the water reminded him of the conversation he'd had with Eve earlier about Alfred Virtue and time travel, and the questions rushed back to his mind. He half-swam to the bank and said to her, "I was wondering: Everard was able to find Robin Hood because I was there to guide him. If I had not been in Havelond, he would have traveled with his father and never talked to Robin."

"So?"

"*So*," Andrew said, "history is changed because I came from our time. It is like that thing you said about ripples on the lake. I came from our part of the lake to *this* part and I am making *new* ripples by being here."

Eve gazed at him and said with true affection, "You are such a *Perry*."

"What does that mean?"

"Your brain works in such a weird way," she said. "The Virtue family has the same problem."

"Am I right? Have I changed history?" he asked.

Eve sat down on a large rock and embraced the silver pitcher on her lap. "All I can tell you is what I read in Alfred Virtue's journal. There was a page where he underlined the phrase, '<u>*Always Remember: You Don't Belong*</u>.'"

"Don't belong?"

"In the past," she said. "We don't belong here, and Time knows it."

"Time *knows*? How does Time know anything?"

"The same way your body knows that something doesn't belong in it," Eve said. "Your body fights to get rid of the foreign invader. If you get a splinter in your thumb, your body isn't going to change much. If you get cancer, your body does *big* things to fight it from changing your body. Alfred Virtue said the same thing is true with Time. We're like splinters in this Time and can get away with little things. But if we try to do something *big*—if we tried to kill the king or burn down London—then that's more like cancer, and Time will counterattack to stop us."

Andrew pushed back into the pool. "That doesn't make sense. How can Time fight to stop anything at all?"

"Maybe that's the wrong way of putting it," she said when he came close again. "The point is, Time *can't* allow us to change the past, just like gravity can't let us fly. It is the way it works, the nature of it. The rules."

Andrew laughed. "Ripples, splinters, gravity, rules . . ."

Eve smiled. "Or maybe it's like wet cement."

Andrew laughed again. "Wet cement?"

Eve said, "Alfred Virtue noted that if you carve your initials into wet cement, the initials slowly dry and get harder and harder to change."

"Unless you have a jackhammer," Andrew said.

"Try to go back in time to change what has already happened and you can't," Eve explained. "You think Everard came to find Robin because you were around to lead him. But it is also possible that he would have come by himself and found Robin on his own."

"Maybe," Andrew said, not convinced. "What if I want to go back in time to stop Adolph Hitler?"

"You won't be able to," she said. "One way or another, Hitler will do what he did. Those initials in the wet cement are dry."

"Yeah, but what if I keep trying?" Andrew challenged her. "What if I am like a jackhammer to Time and . . . and came up with a plan to—?"

Eve cut him off. "The plan would fail and he would go on to do whatever he did the first time. You can't change anything that big."

"How do you know that for sure?" Andrew asked.

"Because Alfred Virtue *tried* and couldn't do it."

Andrew was shocked. He stood up in the pool. "Whoa, wait a minute. Alfred tried to change history?"

"Over and over," she said. "No matter what he did, Time stopped him. And there were a couple of situations when he thought Time was trying to throw him out."

"Throw him out!" Andrew exclaimed. "How did it do that?"

"Alfred wrote how he tried to change the past and suddenly fell sick for no reason. When he persisted, he noticed that bad things happened to him. A large planter fell out of a window and nearly hit him on a street, a horse almost ran him over, a wooden staircase collapsed under him. He realized that Time was trying to get rid of him, just like your body tries to get rid of a virus in your bloodstream. Time fought to keep him from infecting the past. *That's* why he wrote: '*Always Remember: You Don't Belong*.'"

"The whole thing sounds crazy," Andrew said.

Eve laughed. "It *is* crazy. But we're here."

Andrew swam around in a small circle, thinking about it all. He asked, "What about God?"

"God can change whatever he wants," Eve said simply. "Alfred Virtue didn't question that part. I'm sure he didn't want to be at odds with Time *and* God."

Andrew ducked beneath the water again, swimming for the waterfall. He came up and found himself in a small cave behind the waterfall. Reaching up, he grabbed a ledge and pulled himself up.

This would be a great hideout, he thought.

He looked around, wondering if other people in history had found this place. Maybe he'd find a tool or a trinket from some other time.

He saw a small dark something at the far end of the cave, almost hidden in the shadows. Andrew scooted over for a closer look. It was a satchel made of some sort of cloth or leather, with a long strap and a flap over the top. He picked it up. Something inside rattled. Lifting the flap, he found a balled-up tunic, a wooden bowl, an empty water flask, and a leather pouch with three coins. He shoved everything back into the satchel so he could show Eve.

Slipping back into the water, he moved along the ledge to the rock wall. He pushed through the wet curtain of the waterfall. Bushes hid him from the view on the bank and he crouched down into the pool with the idea of lunging out to surprise Eve. Maybe he'd throw the pouch of coins in her direction.

He inched around the bush and saw the rock where she'd been sitting. Next to it, the pitcher lay on its side, the water spilling out.

He looked around, thinking she might be about to do something to scare him instead, but she was nowhere to be seen.

Eve was gone.

Andrew was about to call for Eve, but his instinct told him to wait. He stayed hidden where he was, looking this way and that. Then his eye caught a glint of light near a tree at the crest of the ridge. The light had caught a man's helmet. The wearer was standing and had chain mail on his chest and a long spear in his hands. Even from this distance, Andrew recognized that he was one of Captain Butcher's guards from Nottingham. The man gave a quick look around the stream and disappeared beyond the ridge.

Andrew's mind raced with the possibilities. Was it one guard or a whole army of them? He couldn't imagine just one would venture into the woods, so there had to be more. They must have grabbed Eve. But why were they there? Had they come to rescue Captain Butcher? Were they part of a plan concocted by Sir Reynauld or Sir Alberic to ambush Robin at Thornbridge?

After waiting to be sure the guards had left, Andrew came out of the pool. He retrieved his belt and knife next to the bush and stood soaking wet on the bank, his clothes hanging heavily on his body.

What was he supposed to do?

He had to warn Robin about the guards. But how? They were between him and the outlaws. He wrapped the belt around his waist and touched the hilt of the knife. He couldn't launch an attack on the guards by himself. There must be something else.

An idea came to him and he emptied the satchel he'd found, shoving the contents under the bush. He searched the bank for smooth stones and threw as many as he could into the bag. Slinging it over his shoulder, he crept up the ridge and made his way into the woods.

He saw a dozen guards fanned out ahead, moving slowly forward, with Eve captured in the middle. From the back, he saw a strip of cloth around her head—they'd gagged her—and from the position of her shoulders and arms he assumed they'd bound her hands.

Andrew climbed the nearest tree and, as he'd done with Everard, followed the guards from above. It was hard work to move noiselessly, with his wet clothes, the heavy satchel, and the ache in his side, but somehow his limbs and the limbs of the trees didn't betray him.

He saw the cabin in the thicket off to the right and wondered if anyone there might see the invaders. The guards moved to the left and came to a stop. Three of them conferred, their heads turning together to something he couldn't see. Andrew used the moment to climb as high as he dared.

Through an opening in the branches, he saw what the guards had pointed at: a bridge. Robin and some of the men were on one end of the bridge, looking across to a road beyond. Andrew's gaze followed the road as it snaked in and out of view in the forest. Something glinted in the light and Andrew saw a caravan made up of men on horseback, carts, and people on foot. He had no doubt that it belonged to Sir Reynauld.

Andrew climbed down a few branches and crossed from tree to tree until he was above the gathered guards. They now had their swords drawn and the bowmen readied their bows and arrows. He saw Eve struggling to free her hands. A guard also saw her and backhanded her. She stumbled but stayed on her feet.

Andrew decided to raise the alarm somehow. A shout wouldn't be enough, he knew. He needed to cause a commotion. Reaching into the satchel, he brought out a stone. He moved into position and flicked the stone at Eve, grazing her shoulder. She looked down at the stone, then up at Andrew. Her eyes widened, but she quickly looked away again, so as not to attract the attention of the guards.

Andrew crept from branch to branch, establishing places from which he'd have clear shots and the freedom to move quickly away.

The guards below spread apart. They were about to move again. Andrew took out a stone, aimed carefully and threw hard. The stone hit the helmet of one. Startled, the man spun around to see what had struck him. By then, Andrew had jumped to another branch, throwing another stone and hitting another guard on the shoulder. Soon he had the guards around Eve spinning and turning, trying to figure out what was hitting them, and from where.

From a different branch, Andrew found an angle that allowed the stone to strike a guard next to Eve on the jaw. The throw hurt the guard more than Andrew expected and the man almost lost balance, dropping to his knees. Eve seized the moment to leap onto his back, throwing her bound hands over his helmet and around his neck. This caused even more chaos as the guards now had to deal with the wild waif even as stones rained down on them, seeming from all directions.

Andrew leapt like a squirrel, changing positions again and again. As he reached for the last stone in the satchel, he looked down just as a guard looked up directly at him. An arrow was already notched into his bow. He shouted and let it fly. Andrew leapt away just in time, the arrow striking the branch where his leg had been. He flew with his arms outstretched and caught hold of a branch on the next tree over. But the guards now knew where he was and began to release one arrow after another, splintering the wood and leaves around him.

Just as he prayed that Robin and his men would hear the chaos, a collective roar came from the direction of the bridge, followed by shouts and the buzz of distant arrows. Soon, Andrew heard the heavy clanging of swords.

The guards below were no longer interested in the boy with the stones, so Andrew scampered back to where he'd last seen Eve. He hoped that she'd somehow escaped and was now hiding up in a tree.

He let out a startled gasp. Eve was lying between a bush and a tree, as if she'd been carelessly thrown there. A helmet sat next to her.

Andrew dropped down next to her. He shrugged off the satchel and used his knife to cut the bonds from her hands. As he pulled the gag away from her mouth, she slowly opened her eyes.

"Ouch," she groaned. "He hit me on the side of the head. What kind of man hits a girl?"

"Maybe the kind that has a girl on his back with her hands around his neck," Andrew said. "Can you stand up?"

She nodded. He helped her to her feet.

There was a crunch of leaves behind Andrew. He heard a low "aha" and saw Eve's eyes widen.

Instinctively, Andrew grabbed the helmet and spun around as fast and hard as he could. The heavy piece of metal served as a solid weapon against the guard who was coming at him with his hands outstretched. The helmet caught him on the side of his bare head. He fell, hitting the other side of his head against a tree. Dazed, he slid to his hands and knees.

"We have to go," Eve said and took Andrew's hand. They stumbled at first, found their footing, and sprinted away from the guard and the fighting nearby.

"You were pretty good with those rocks," Eve said when they reached a safe space behind a tall line of bushes.

"I'll bet he wished he had kept his helmet on," Andrew said.

"I pulled that off when he was trying to throw me off of his back," Eve explained.

The two of them paused to catch their breath. It was only a few minutes, but they both realized at the same time how quiet the woods had become. They slowly stood up to see what had become of the battle, but the battle was finished. Robin's men were leading the Nottingham guards back to the bridge.

"We won," Andrew said.

"All thanks to you," said Eve. She touched his arm. "We can go home now, if you want." Her hand went to the chain around her neck.

"And miss the ending? I don't think so."

They scrambled to catch up to the outlaws and their captives.

"How dare you miscreants attack the sheriff's guards! I defy you. I swear by all the saints that your heads will rot on pikes!" Andrew recognized the voice as Captain Butcher's. Robin had brought him from wherever he'd been kept and now placed him with his captured guards in a line near the bridge.

Robin stepped over to him, a smile on his face. "Why do you complain, good captain? Your men are alive. And we have fed you and kept you in greater comfort than even the sheriff himself afforded you." The outlaw put a gag over the captain's mouth. "Be watchful now. Bear witness in silence."

Andrew and Eve moved under a tree, waiting to see what Robin would do next.

Robin saw them and saluted. "Is it true that I am to thank you for this?" He waved a hand at the captured guards.

Eve hooked a thumb at Andrew. "He saved the day."

Robin strode over and took Andrew's hand, giving it a hardy shake. "Lad, I am indebted to you yet again."

Andrew nodded. "You are welcome," was all he could think to say.

"Why were they here?" Eve asked the outlaw.

"I was careless," said Robin. "A tradesman from Nottingham recognized the captain when we carted him from Ravenswood, and he followed us. I was sure the tradesman was a friend and paid him no mind. The tradesman, thinking he would receive a reward, returned to Nottingham and told the guards. They came to rescue their beloved captain." Robin shot a look at Captain Butcher, who continued to glare at him. "It would have served them better to think through their plan of attack. Poor training on the part of their captain, I think."

The captain snorted at him and turned away.

Robin said to Eve, "I bid you, my waif, to return to Reuben and his daughter in the cabin. Two men guard on the outside, but I would have you inside, since they find great comfort from you."

Eve cast a disappointed look at the bridge but said, "Aye, Master Robin." She gave a quick nod to Andrew and walked away.

"Now to business," Robin said to Andrew and went to the bridge, calling out final orders to his gathered men.

Sir Reynauld's caravan was now in view, slowly making its way forward. A single rider on horseback at the head carried a red banner adorned with the image of a white tower and, above it, a bird descending with its talons outstretched. Behind the bearer rode Sir Reynauld and Sir Alberic, side by side, both in chain mail and tunics. Sir Reynauld's tunic was decorated with a coat of arms identical to the banner. Sir Alberic's tunic was a simple white with a red sash cutting across at an angle. Behind them trailed another half-dozen men on horses, several horse-drawn carts with servants and crates, and, finally, the servants on foot.

Andrew wondered where Robin was keeping Everard and Maurice, and why he hadn't brought them to the bridge yet.

Sir Reynauld held up his hand and the caravan came to a halt on the far side of the bridge. He dismounted, as did Sir Alberic, and the two men crossed with heavy steps to the midway point.

Robin spoke to Little John and Warren the Bowman, who were positioned at the foot of the bridge on the outlaw side. Someone in a hooded cloak stepped from behind a tree and walked with Robin to meet the two knights. As they drew close to the center of the bridge, the hooded man pushed back his head cover. It was Everard.

Sir Reynauld gave his son a scornful look. "Am I betrayed by my own flesh and blood?"

"Nay, Father," said Everard. "I am here in good faith to avoid bloodshed."

Sir Reynauld looked at Robin Hood as he asked Everard, "Has the scoundrel bewitched you? Are you now another rogue among his outlaws in the Greenwood?"

"I am not, though there are worse things I could become," Everard countered.

Sir Reynauld grunted. "Why are you here, then?"

Everard cleared his throat and said in a formal tone, "My lord Father, promise to yield Havelond and we shall depart safely with Maurice. I have the word of Robin Hood."

"The word of this man is of no value to me," said Sir Reynauld. "However, *my* word is that I will skin his carcass for the birds."

Robin calmly asked, "You are unrepentant for your evil deeds, Sir Reynauld?"

"I will not repent for you, outlaw."

Robin turned to Sir Alberic. "What say you, Sir Alberic?"

"What would you have me say?" Sir Alberic responded.

Robin laughed. "I see you glancing back at the road as if you expect someone. Might it be the sheriff's guards from Nottingham, who you will see bound on the other side of the bridge, should you crane your neck to look?"

Sir Alberic looked at Captain Butcher and the guards. He gazed at Robin with an expression of indifference. "They are nothing to do with me."

"No?" Robin asked, a tone of amusement in his voice. "Perhaps you are looking for your allies from York?"

Sir Alberic's face twitched.

Robin continued, "Alas, your messenger, good man that he is, never reached York to deliver your message. However, he has been treated kindly and given a hearty meal for his troubles."

"You are without honor, every one of you!" Sir Reynauld shouted, his face matching the red in his coat of arms. "Give me but a chance and I shall show you—" Faster than anyone would have thought possible, Reynauld's hand went to the knife in his belt and, quick as lightning, had it drawn and thrusting toward Robin.

Everard shouted, "Father!" and stepped between his father and the outlaw.

The knife plunged deep into the young man's chest. He fell into Robin and sunk to his knees. Sir Reynauld reared back, the bloody knife in his hand. His face filled with the horror of what he'd done. He dropped the knife and it fell off of the bridge into the river.

Little John rushed to Robin's side. Warren the Bowman had his arrow notched and ready to shoot.

"Vile!" Sir Reynauld cried out and knelt next to his son. His face was twisted in anguish and anger. "I shall be avenged of this before my eyes close in death."

Robin looked at the man, astonished. "Avenged, Sir Reynauld? 'Twas your knife that has done this evil deed. Turn it on yourself if you seek to avenge him."

Sir Reynauld spat at the outlaw.

Robin ignored the insolence and said, "Save the life of your remaining son. Promise now and forever to yield Havelond and leave its true owners in peace."

Sir Reynauld stood up. "Hear me, knave. I shall see you and your men hanged for this." He took a few steps back and only then did Andrew realize that Sir Alberic had already retreated to the far end of the bridge. Sir Reynauld pulled the sword from its sheath and lifted it.

Too late did Warren the Bowman realize that the sword wasn't for Robin but was a signal of some sort. He let fly an arrow that struck Sir Reynauld in the arm. The sword flew from Sir Reynauld's hands, hitting the rail of the bridge and joining the knife in the water below.

"Attack!" Sir Reynauld yelled, clutching the arrow in his arm and rushing back across the bridge.

A horn sounded from somewhere in the caravan. The servants in the carts, sitting passively until now, leapt to their feet. They cast aside their rough robes and tunics to reveal chain mail. Swords, spears, and bows seemed to come from nowhere. The servants at the back of the caravan drew knives and lifted up spears. Over two dozen men now rushed to the bridge.

"Back!" Robin shouted to Little John as he grabbed Everard and, with surprising strength, lifted the dead man onto his shoulder and carried him to the outlaw's side of the bridge. He crossed to Andrew and put Everard down at the base of the tree. "See to him," Robin said, dashing back to the bridge to meet the oncoming assault.

Andrew was puzzled, wondering why Robin wanted him to watch over a dead body. Then he saw Everard's eyes twitch and open wide, ablaze with fright and pain. He took a deep, wheezing breath and thrashed his arms as if defending himself.

"Calm down!" Andrew said and suddenly thought of all the movies he'd ever seen where someone had been wounded. "I need to stop the bleeding," Andrew said.

"Allow me to help." A figure came near and knelt on the other side of Everard. It was a young man with curly hair. "I am Father Simon," he said. He pushed the sleeves up on his black robe. Grabbing the knife from Andrew's belt, he deftly cut at Everard's clothes. He soon had Everard's bare chest exposed, revealing a severe gash on the right side of his rib cage.

The priest cut the sleeve from Everard's robe and pressed the cloth against the wound. Everard cried out.

An arrow suddenly buzzed between Andrew and the priest, slamming into the tree behind them. If Everard had been sitting up, he'd have been struck and killed.

"Lift his feet," Father Simon said, grabbing under Everard's arms. The two of them carried Everard behind the tree and lay him down again. Father Simon worked again on the wound.

Andrew peeked around the tree to see the Battle of Thornbridge in all of its savagery.

Robin had allowed many of Sir Reynauld's men to cross the bridge so the band of outlaws would have the full advantage of their positions in and around the trees. Arrows flew like a swarm of angry wasps, swords rang against one another, spears and staffs parlayed, shouts and cries punctuated successes and failures.

Sir Reynauld was in the thick of it, the arrow broken in his right arm. He swung another sword with his left, raging at Robin's men like a wild animal.

Sir Alberic was back on the bridge, not fighting at all, but making his way slowly through those who were.

"What is he doing?" Andrew asked no one.

"Hold this," Father Simon called out behind him.

Andrew turned. The priest gestured to the cloth on Everard's chest. Andrew knelt and pressed the cloth on the wound while Father Simon shoved his hands under his robes. He brought out a small pouch, undid the string that held it closed, and retrieved a vial. He yanked out the stopper and poured oil on his fingers. He marked the Sign of the Cross on Everard's forehead.

He leaned close to Everard's face and, in Latin, whispered, "*In nomine Patris, et Filii, et Spiritus Sancti* . . . Everard, son of Sir Reynauld of Prestbury . . ." Everard nodded once or twice, and said, "Aye." Then, in English, Father Simon said, "By God's grace, we will carry you to a place where I may properly treat you."

Father Simon looked at Andrew with sorrowful eyes and put the stopper in the vial, tucking it away again. "We need help carrying him," he said, and he rushed off to find it.

Everard's hand suddenly took hold of Andrew's. "I beg you, take me to my brother ere I die. He must be told . . ." His voice trailed off.

"Told what?" Andrew asked.

"Told . . . there is no glory in our pride, only eternal pain . . . beg him to yield . . ." His hand relaxed in Andrew's. He closed his eyes, his chest rising as he drew in a harsh breath of air. Then he slowly exhaled.

Andrew heard a terrible rattling sound coming from somewhere inside of the young man. He waited for him to breathe in again, but he didn't and never would.

Andrew lowered his head. Tears formed in his eyes and spilled hot down his cheeks.

The battle subsided as Sir Reynauld's men were slowly defeated. Robin's men rounded them up to join Captain Butcher and his guards. Sir Reynauld himself had collapsed due to the loss of blood from his wound and now had a second arrow in his side. Father Simon bent over him to administer first aid, but the obstinate man pushed him away.

A question slowly worked its way through the Men of the Greenwood: where is Sir Alberic?

The prevailing answer was that the coward had run for York.

Andrew wasn't so sure. He remembered his last glimpse of Sir Alberic, slipping past the fighters on the bridge. Maybe he was hiding behind a tree, waiting for a chance to attack Robin. The thought made Andrew nervous enough to make his way past the prisoners and the bridge to the part of the woods Sir Alberic had fled. Walking along the road, he searched to the left and the right, hoping for any clues about the praying mantis's whereabouts.

He heard a groan and stopped. Through the trees, a lone figure was crouching low to the ground. Andrew raced toward it, pulling his knife from his belt. Coming closer, he saw that it was Ket the Troll crouching down next to one of Robin's men.

"Ket?" Andrew asked.

"He is still alive," Ket said, his hand on the man's head. "He's been stripped of most of his clothes. Why, pray tell, would someone take a man's clothes in the heat of battle?"

"It was Sir Alberic," Andrew said.

"He disguised himself to escape?" Ket asked.

Andrew had an alarming thought. "Not to escape, but to do what he came to do. I know where he is!"

Together, Eve, Reuben, and Ruth had been praying. The battle was a distant commotion, but that did no less to calm the fears of the old man and his daughter. They worried all the more when Dodd, son of Alstan, told them that he and the other guards were leaving to join the conflict.

Eve had bolted the door and shuttered the two windows.

Less than an hour had gone by when they noticed the clamor had ceased.

"It is finished," Ruth said, relieved.

"Who won?" asked Reuben, worried.

From the door came a gentle knock.

Eve called out, "Who is there?"

"Thomas the Tanner," the voice said. "The battle is won. Robin bids you to come, with all your belongings."

Reuben said, "Thanks be to God."

Ruth clasped her hands and closed her eyes, whispering the same.

"Open up," Thomas the Tanner said. "Master Robin is waiting."

Eve hesitated. She was suspicious. She had never heard of Thomas the Tanner.

"Please, dear girl, do not keep him waiting," Reuben said to Eve, gesturing to the door.

She undid the bolt.

Thomas the Tanner slouched into the cabin. He was draped in a long cloak that hung as if it was too large for his body. His face was obscured by a hood. "My thanks, dear child," he said.

"I have never seen you before," Eve said.

"You are unlikely to have ever seen me," the tanner said. "My face is horribly disfigured, owing to the treachery of Sir Alberic and his evil hordes. I keep to myself, even among the Men of the Greenwood."

The explanation sounded reasonable. Eve relaxed.

"Gather all your things," Thomas the Tanner said. "Today we shall have justice."

Reuben's face filled with gratitude and he knelt next to a small trunk. He opened the lid and began to rearrange what few belongings they had inside. "Bring me the candlesticks," he said to his daughter.

Ruth picked up two silver candlesticks from a side table and handed them to him.

"Take only what you most cherish," the tanner said, with a hint of impatience. "Religious items, as you will. Any legal documents . . ."

The tanner's emphasis on "legal documents" caught Eve's attention.

Reuben shuffled the clothing and keepsakes, then brought out several bound parchments. Some bore wax seals.

"Ah," said the tanner as the old man placed the parchments on the floor next to him. The tanner's hands slowly rose to his chest. He rubbed them together, the left inside the right, then the right inside the left, and the thin fingers intertwining and coming loose again.

At that moment, Eve thought of a praying mantis, and she remembered what Andrew had said about Sir Alberic.

Reuben looked up and must have realized the same, for he cleared his throat nervously and put a protective hand over the ledgers, pulling them protectively back to himself.

"Now sir," the tanner said, his voice oozing with assurance, "those are the very documents you must give to me for safekeeping."

"Thank you, kind man. I shall hold these close," said Reuben, standing with the ledgers clutched tightly.

Ruth heard the change in her father's tone and now stood erect, a puzzled look on her face.

The man's shoulders stiffened. "I insist," he said, and shoved his hood back with one hand, while the other emerged from inside his cloak with a long knife. All doubt was gone. Sir Alberic himself stood before them.

Ruth shrieked and Reuben stepped back, pushing his daughter behind him.

Eve used the distraction to seize a quarterstaff that one of the outlaws left leaning against the wall. Her practice

with Robin's men paid off as she used both hands to
bring the staff level, then thrust it at Sir Alberic, hitting
him solidly with the blunt end on the side of the head.
He howled as he reeled back but recovered quickly and
lunged forward with the knife pointed her way. Cat-like,
she jumped aside, swinging the staff around, hitting him
in the shoulder.

"Run!" Eve shouted at Reuben and Ruth. But the old
man and his daughter were too slow getting around Sir
Alberic to the door.

The evil knight leapt between them and their escape,
brandishing the knife again. "The deeds!" he commanded.
"Place them in my hand now and you may live."

"I do not believe you," Eve said, gripping the staff for a
renewed attack.

As she thrust forward, Sir Alberic swung his free arm and
knocked the staff off its course. Eve lost her balance and
tumbled forward. Sir Alberic brought his knife-wielding
hand around to stab at her as she fell, but Reuben threw
himself forward, using the ledgers to swat Alberic's arm.

The knife flew from Alberic's hand as Eve hit the ground
on her side, losing her grip on the staff. Alberic kicked at
her, his foot catching the side of her head. A burst of light
flashed, followed by a sharp pain.

Alberic, with surprising dexterity, swung his elbow
back, hitting Reuben in the chest. The old man staggered
backward, knocking Ruth to the side and landing hard
against the opposite wall.

Eve saw Alberic's knife only a few feet away and rolled to grab it. He kicked at her again, catching her arm. Grabbing her by the scruff of her neck, he jerked her to her knees. "I shall have those deeds, whether you are dead or alive. Beginning with you," he said to Eve. He grabbed the knife from the floor and held it near her throat.

"Mercy!" Ruth cried out.

Eve braced herself. She had wondered if it was possible to die in the past and feared she would now find out. A prayer went through her mind, interrupted by a thin whistling sound that was quickly followed by a dull thud. She felt Sir Alberic's hold on her release as he let out a fierce cry and stumbled a few steps. Eve dove away from him, crab-crawling across the floor to Reuben and Ruth. A small stone skittered nearby and she knew immediately what had happened.

Sir Alberic's hand pressed against his forehead, a trickle of blood sliding through his fingers. He had a dazed expression and muttered, "By the saints." He looked at his bloody hand.

Another stone whistled through the open window and slammed into the wall to his left. He jerked his head toward the sound, holding up the knife as if it would protect him somehow.

Another stone rocketed in, striking him hard on his right shoulder. Realizing the assault was coming through the open window, he dropped to his knees to take cover.

Only a few feet away, the ledgers lay where Reuben had dropped them. Sir Alberic now reached for them, his face a picture of greed.

Eve made as if to jump at Alberic, but Reuben caught her arm.

He gave Eve a grim look and shook his head.

Sir Alberic reached up for the latch. Another stone hit just above his head. He flinched but was undaunted in his escape. Yanking the door open, he climbed to his feet. Eve heard a sharp buzzing sound and Alberic screamed, falling onto his side, the ledgers tumbling away. He clutched his leg. A small black arrow jutted out from above his knee.

Ket the Troll stepped into view, a fresh arrow in his bow pointed at Sir Alberic.

"God be praised," Reuben said.

"Amen," Eve whispered and picked up the fallen ledgers, handing them to Reuben.

Sir Alberic snarled at Ket, "I am in agony."

"'Tis only the start," Ket warned.

Andrew appeared in the doorway, next to Ket. His eyes darted around the room until they caught Eve. "Are you all right?"

"You missed with two of your throws," she said.

He looked indignant. "I did that on purpose!" he said.

Voices outside told her that more of Robin's men had come. She took a deep breath, hoping to calm her pounding heart.

Reuben and Ruth, huddling together, prayed, "O give thanks unto God for he is good and his mercy endures forever . . ."

Two of Robin's men carried Sir Alberic to the bridge. Father Simon made efforts to treat the man's wounded knee. The Men of the Greenwood came from their different positions in the forest, bringing more captives.

Sir Reynauld lay among his captured men, a long arrow rising from his side. His face was a sickly pale color and his eyes were closed. Maurice, Sir Reynauld's remaining son, sat propped up on a makeshift carrier nearby. His right leg was bandaged and pressed between two wooden planks that served as splints. Will Scarlet stood close by, a hand on the hilt of the Spanish knife in his belt.

The members of Sir Reynauld's household who had not fought now sat in a nearby thicket. Robin had ordered food and drink for them. Captain Butcher and his guards were still bound and sat in a dusty patch under the sun. The captain was gagged, though there was no hiding his frown beneath the cloth.

The dead—of which there were two among Robin's men and seven among Sir Reynauld's—were taken to another part of the forest where prayers would be offered and burials undertaken.

Andrew and Eve found a place to sit under a broad tree at the edge of the crowd.

"What will Robin do?" Andrew asked.

"Put an end to it," Eve replied.

Robin Hood, his clothes dirty and stained from the battle, strode to the center of the gathering. "We thank God for his mercy today," he said. "Now we pray for his wisdom and justice."

Sir Reynauld opened his eyes, a look of raw malice filling them. The hatred there said more than any words Sir Reynauld could have expressed. He sullenly glanced from face to face, landing on his son's, who returned a similar look.

Robin looked down upon Sir Reynauld and said, "You are dying, Sir Reynauld. Your wound cannot be mended by anyone here. For the sake of your soul, speak to our good priest. Repent of your sins."

Sir Reynauld glared at the outlaw. "I will appeal for no mercy from you, vermin! Outlaw! Wolf's head! Runaway rogue!" The words were mere sputterings that ended in a sharp gasp from a sudden spasm of pain. His back arched and he slumped to one side, his eyes now staring, drained of his hate-filled life.

"This is justice," Robin said and performed the Sign of the Cross.

Maurice grabbed both sides of the carrier, shaking it as he let out a piercing cry of anguish. "As God is my witness, you will pay for this," he railed at Robin. "How it will be accomplished, I do not know. But I shall have revenge against you."

Robin gazed at Maurice. "Against me?" he asked and crouched next to the dead man. He pointed to the arrow in Sir Reynauld's side. "The colors on this arrow are not mine, nor of any man in my service."

Maurice looked at him doubtfully.

"Do you not recognize it?" Robin asked him. "This arrow belongs to the house of Havelond."

"By the black rood," Maurice shouted, "how is that possible? Has Bennett come to the battle?"

"Nay, he still remains bedridden from the beating your men gave him," Robin said, his tone of accusation clear.

"To what rogue does that arrow belong?" Maurice demanded.

Robin's men shuffled, stepping aside as Lady Anne passed through them. "It belongs to me," she said. "I am the rogue."

Maurice was astonished. "You?"

She stood in front of him, her hands clasped tightly in front of her. "Your father, dishonorable man that he was, stood ready to slay Warren the Bowman while his back was turned. I let fly the arrow to stop him. Glad I am to see the end of the accursed man."

Maurice's face contorted with rage. "Then, with all of my might, I shall seek my revenge against you, my lady."

"By all the saints!" Robin cried out and stormed over to Maurice. "Have you not lost enough?"

Maurice recoiled, though his look remained defiant.

Robin leaned in until his face was only inches away from the man's. "By God's grace, you have been given many warnings this day. Your family begat this tragedy when you sought to steal Havelond from this good lady and her noble husband. To worsen your sin, you set cruel men to kill Bennett for no reason other than to possess what was not yours. Has the death of your brother, who sought to right your wrongs, not taught you anything? Has the death of your father, prideful and unrepentant, not shown you the folly of your days if you do not change your heart? I spared your life at Prestbury for this very purpose: to allow you to repent."

Maurice flinched at Robin's words but said nothing.

Robin raised a hand as a signal. Little John and Dodd carried out the body of Everard and laid it next to Sir Reynauld.

Maurice groaned and turned away. There was a loud hitch in his breath of a stifled sob.

"See the end of your days!" Robin said to him. "Will you repent or not? If not, I shall give Will Scarlet leave to satisfy his own vengeance upon you for the wrongs you committed against him in Nottingham and Ravenswood."

Will drew his knife.

Andrew suddenly raised his hand, as if he were at school, and walked forward. "Master Robin!"

Robin turned, surprised by the boy's interruption. "Speak, young Andrew."

"I have a message for Maurice."

Maurice looked affronted. "What message could a *beggar* have for me?"

"Everard's own words, spoken to me as he died."

All eyes were on him now. He could feel his face turning red. He hated giving oral reports at school. He felt his mouth go dry now. "He wanted you to know that there is no glory in your pride, only eternal pain. He said to beg you to yield.'"

Maurice's face fell. "What is this trickery?"

"They were his last words," Andrew said. "I swear."

"The boy would not lie," Robin said. "Indeed, your brother's heart speaks the truth that, had you and your father embraced, we would have been saved from today's suffering."

Maurice's body slumped as if the thing that held it so rigid had been suddenly taken away. He put his hands over his face and muttered something.

"Speak again," Robin said.

Maurice's hands came away from his face, the dust of the day now smeared by his tears. "For the love of my brother, I yield," he said.

Robin looked relieved. He pointed at Captain Butcher. "Bear witness, Captain, to what you have heard!"

The captain tried to speak through his gag, but it only came out as muffled complaints.

"For the sake of justice," Robin announced, "all of Sir Reynauld's belongings in Havelond, and those of any value in the carts, shall be given as compensation for the trouble he has given to Lady Anne and her husband Bennett of Havelond."

Lady Anne, still standing nearby, said, "Nay, dear cousin, I want none of his belongings, nor anything that will remind me of these dark days."

Robin nodded. "I understand, my lady," he said. "However, you *will* keep the box of treasure we discovered in Sir Reynauld's possessions." It was not a request.

Lady Anne bowed and curtsied to him.

"I, then, have nothing," Maurice said.

"You have your life," Robin countered. "You have the generous offer of your father's property from Lady Anne."

"Where shall I put it? I have nowhere to live," he said, now sulking.

"You have the gamekeeper's cottage on the grounds of Prestbury," Robin said. "We saved it from the burning."

"A cottage?" Maurice said.

"'Tis not the grandeur you believe you deserve," Robin said with strained patience. "Remember how this good lady lived in a much smaller cottage while you feasted in her home. Be grateful!"

Maurice folded his arms and said no more.

Done with him, Robin now turned and called out, "Where is the vile and oppressive knight who gave generously to our grief on this day? Sir Alberic de Wisgar!"

Sir Alberic was propped up on the rail of the bridge, one of Robin's men on each side. His leg was bandaged and soiled with blood. With an overdramatic show, he pushed the men away. "I shall stand on my own," he said. They let him go and moved aside. Sir Alberic swayed, then fell to the ground with a cry of pain.

The crowd laughed.

"Just as well," Robin said to him. He nodded to Dodd, who had been standing at the edge of the crowd. Dodd retreated and, a moment later, brought forward Reuben and his daughter, accompanied by Ket the Troll and four other outlaws.

Ruth cast a shy glance around the assembly and suddenly caught sight of the face of Alberic. She retreated, backing into her father, holding him with both hands.

"Reuben of Stamford," Robin called out, "is this the man you know to have incited the mob and attacked your people at York?"

"Aye," replied the old man. "By his command, men, women, and even little children were grievously injured so he might be released from his great debt to me."

Robin gazed down at Sir Alberic. "You attacked the cathedral, as well. For that, evil knight, you will suffer more punishment than I may impose upon you here."

Sir Alberic looked up at Robin with cold eyes.

"What are we to do with him?" Robin asked the crowd.

Cries came out to hang the man; others wanted him whipped; still others called for him to be drawn and quartered.

"I am a knight of the realm!" Sir Alberic snarled. "I will not be judged by peasants. The law demands that I—"

"Do not speak to me of the law, Sir Alberic!" Robin shouted. "You bend the laws with a breathtaking impunity. Do you invoke them now to escape punishment? Coward! My purpose here is one of *justice*, not adherence to your unjust laws!"

Captain Butcher squirmed and tried to shout through his gag.

Robin held up his hand. "Hear me! There are two matters to which we attend. The first is the debt owed by Sir Alberic to Reuben of Stamford. Are you prepared to repay the money, Sir Alberic?"

"Are you mad?" Sir Alberic said. "I would not carry such a treasure with me."

"Where is it stored?"

Sir Alberic hesitated to answer.

"Do not test me," Robin warned.

"'Tis safely kept at my estate," Sir Alberic said. "Send me to fetch it."

Robin laughed. "Deceitful creature that you are, I am sure that if I were to allow you to leave this forest, you would renew your efforts to slay the one to whom your debt is owed. Reuben and his family will not be safe as long as you owe him the money." Robin paused, giving the man a stern look. "For that reason, I have transferred your debt from Reuben of Stamford to *me*."

Sir Alberic blinked as if he did not understand what Robin had said. "To you?"

"I have paid Reuben from my own treasure," Robin said. "You must now repay *me* the debt you once owed to him."

"Why?" Sir Alberic asked.

"You will not bully nor hound me as you have this poor man. I shall collect it from you forthwith."

Sir Alberic suddenly laughed. "You have been declared an outlaw! I am under no obligation to pay you."

"According to your law," Robin said.

"According to *the* law," Sir Alberic repeated.

"I have stated my views upon your law," Robin reminded him. "Look now upon the body of Sir Reynauld. Think also of his estate at Prestbury, burned to the ground. Do you doubt that I shall collect the debt from you?"

Sir Alberic slowly shook his head.

"This very day, we will send messengers to your family to return henceforth with the money you owe," Robin announced. "Or know, wicked man, that you will not leave this forest alive."

Sir Alberic went pale. "You would not dare."

Robin gave him a cruel smile. "Will you wager your life to find out?"

Again, Sir Alberic shook his head.

"Once we have settled the first matter, we will attend to the second matter," Robin said.

"What second matter?" Sir Alberic demanded.

"The crimes you committed against the people of York—the wanton destruction, the invasion of the cathedral," Robin said.

"You cannot judge me for those!" Sir Alberic shouted.

"I can, but I will not," Robin said. "I have not met him as yet, but I believe Sir Lawrence of Raby, the marshal of the king's justice, is a stern but honest man. Unlike the sheriff of York, he does not take bribes nor partake in the corruption of Sir Guy of Gisborne, the knights of Wrangby castle, nor even of you, Sir Alberic, though you have made every attempt. To him you will be delivered. By *his* judgment, as the appointed marshal of our good king, justice shall be rendered. A hanging, I suspect."

Sir Alberic's face went from a pale white to a sickly green. *Just like a praying mantis*, Andrew thought.

Robin gestured to Little John. "Take him away for safekeeping."

"Aye, Master Robin," Little John said. He grabbed Sir Alberic by the arm and pulled him up. The last Andrew saw of the praying mantis man, he was being half-carried, half-dragged, into the woods.

Before the end of the day, riders from Nottingham arrived at Thornbridge. Leading them was Silas, son of Reuben, along with armed men ready to escort Reuben and Ruth to greater safety. Andrew heard them mention the town of Godmanchester as a haven for their people. Their reunion was sweet and full of grateful tears.

At their goodbye, Reuben clasped Andrew's hand and said, "God's blessings be upon you, brave boy." He embraced Eve and gave her a silver ring. "'Tis only a small token of my gratitude," he said.

Over the next two days, it was joked among Robin's men that the children of Sir Alberic hotly debated whether or not to pay their father's debt. Apparently, greed ran deep in the family and they were willing to let him die to keep their treasure. Sir Alberic sent a renewed appeal, with threats and promises and a reminder that Robin would collect from them with or without their cooperation. It was enough to persuade them, and the amount was delivered to Robin by the end of the third day.

Sir Alberic was taken by a party of Robin's men to the king's marshal, Sir Lawrence of Raby. Jenkins, who had been held prisoner in Ravenswood since his capture, was also handed over. It was later reported that Sir Lawrence, well aware of the knight's terrible deeds in York, was more than ready to dispense the king's justice.

Later, Andrew heard it said that the Battle of Thornbridge, as some called it, was told as a legend throughout the countryside. The legends included stories of a boy who, like the shepherd David in the Bible, wielded stones to bring down evil men, and a girl with magical eyes who saved an old Jew and his daughter from great harm.

Word returned that men and women breathed freely again to know that men as evil as Sir Alberic de Wisgar and Sir Reynauld of Prestbury had met true justice. Robin's reputation for brave and good deeds spread far and wide.

Andrew and Eve agreed they were ready to go home and found the perfect way to go when Robin asked them to help with one more task.

Robin organized a party of men, led by Robin himself, to escort Lady Anne and her husband Bennett back to Havelond. Andrew and Eve were asked by Robin to join the caravan. "You are good for her spirits," he said to them quietly.

Lady Anne thanked her cousin profusely for all he had done. "I beg you, dear Robin," she said, "permit me to return the favor, any favor of any kind, to show my gratitude."

Robin bowed to her, "With pleasure, good lady. I shall remember, should the time ever come."

The journey was long, since Bennett had to be carried in a covered cart, traveling slowly to ease his discomfort. Andrew saw the man only once, when they placed him into the cart on a bed made of a goose down mattress. Bennett wore bandages on his head and across the side of his swollen face.

Andrew heard that Bennett had awakened just once since his beating. He held his wife's hand. "My darling," he had whispered before falling to sleep again. Lady Anne believed that, by the help of the Blessed Mother and all the saints, Bennett would recover, though it would take months, perhaps years. Andrew wanted to believe it too.

The manor at Havelond looked different now that Sir Reynauld was gone. Maybe it was Andrew's imagination, but he thought it seemed brighter, the stones themselves aglow with sunlight.

It became clear that Sir Reynauld did not really believe he'd have to vacate the place. The carts he had used in the caravan were filled with his mercenary soldiers, the treasure to pay them, and crates stuffed with mostly junk. The house still contained his more valued possessions, which Lady Anne promised to send away immediately.

Lady Anne stood in the dining hall and wept with joy to be home again. "There is much I must do to free this house from the sinful hold Sir Reynauld had upon it," she said. "I will have endless days of joyful work."

"While you are at it," Andrew said to her, "you have a leak in one of your closets."

Andrew and Eve were about to leave, making it as far as the courtyard by the stable, when Robin caught up to them.

"Where are you going?" he asked.

"Into the woods," Eve replied. "We may practice stone-throwing, to improve Andrew's aim."

"Hey!" Andrew protested.

"A worthy endeavor," Robin said. He suddenly gave them both affectionate embraces, as if he knew he may not see them again. "Thank you for saving my life and the lives of my men, which I am reminded you did on more than one occasion."

Andrew blushed and Eve smiled.

The outlaw stood at the gate and watched them as they crossed the field to the woods.

Andrew's mind went back to the day he'd first arrived and how unreal it felt then. Even now, he wasn't sure whether or not this was all just a dream.

As they came closer to the cave, Andrew asked, "What happened to him? Alfred Virtue, I mean."

"He disappeared," Eve said.

"That's it? He just disappeared?"

"He went on an expedition and disappeared," she said.

"Maybe he's still alive," Andrew said. "It's like that rule in all the stories: if there is no body, then the character is probably not dead."

Eve laughed. "He would be a hundred and fifty years old by now."

"Maybe he figured out how to slow down time for his body," Andrew suggested. "He might be a hundred and fifty in our time but, in another time, he might be only forty, or twenty."

Eve shook her head. "I think we age in the same way, no matter what time we're in."

"Are you sure? What if we don't go back to our time for twenty years?" Andrew asked, thinking of the children in *The Chronicles of Narnia*. "Will we show up right after we left, but look twenty years older? How does that work?"

Eve groaned. "I don't know. It gives me a headache to think about."

Andrew had more questions, but he didn't ask them. He hoped to read Alfred Virtue's writings once they returned. He had a lot to learn.

They retrieved their clothes from behind the bushes and got dressed in their modern outfits. Andrew thought his jeans and shirt felt strange: a little too loose and too soft, not rugged enough. His sneakers didn't fit as comfortably as they had before. Maybe his callouses had made his feet bigger. He wondered how he would explain it all to his parents.

"Ready?" Eve said and pulled out the necklace.

"Ready," Andrew said, but he held up his hand. "Wait."

"What's wrong?" she asked.

Andrew was looking at a tree nearby. He called out, "I see you, Ket the Troll! Come down!"

The troll dropped from the tree. "Your eyes are sharper than they were, Master Andrew," he said.

Eve looked at Andrew nervously, then asked Ket, "What are you doing here?"

He gazed at her for a moment. "We trolls know greater mysteries of the world than ever we tell. I have believed, from the first moment I saw you, good waif, and you, lad, that you were not of this world. I wonder how it is so."

Eve presented the case to him, showing him the stone and explaining what she knew about it. Andrew noticed that she didn't mention exactly where the stone was about to take them, only that they would go away to another land. He assumed any explanation about time travel would be too long and involved.

Eve finished and Ket nodded his shaggy head. "The stone is well known in our legends," he said.

"You know about it?" Andrew asked.

"Aye. I know the whereabouts of others like it."

Surprised, Andrew and Eve looked at each other.

"We'd love to see them," Eve said.

"Perhaps, as God wills," Ket said. "Until then, your secret is safe with me." The troll gave them a low and respectful bow. He turned and walked away, disappearing quickly into the trees as he always seemed to do.

Eve took Andrew's hand and they stepped behind the ivy curtain. A rock wall faced them until Eve touched the Radiant Stone, and a new opening appeared. They stepped through.

For the complete story of Robin Hood and his adventures, listen to *The Legends of Robin Hood*, a six-hour audio drama from the Augustine Institute featuring over 60 acclaimed British actors, full production of sound, and original music.

Go to airtheatre.org to find out more.